FALLING FOR ZEKE

A SWEET ROMANTIC SUSPENSE

SARA BLACKARD

For Shelly and Jodi
Thank you for cheering me on.
For the countless hours reading really rough drafts.
For the belly laughs and the thousands of texts.
I couldn't do this without you.

CHAPTER ONE

Zeke Greene growled low and dangerous at his screen, tempted beyond reason to pull the hidden Glock from beneath the desktop and blow the entire computer to smithereens. As a member of the highly trained special ops unit of the army, he'd led secret missions into the deepest, darkest pits of the world. He'd rescued victims from sex trafficking, protected different government officials through dangerous situations, and tracked terrorists through the belly of the beast. Since leaving the army, he'd started his security firm, Stryker Security, and gathered the best men he knew—his brothers-in-arms—his family. From their growing client list, they must do a decent job. So why couldn't he figure out how to slay the monster known as QuickBooks?

He grabbed the sides of the laptop and shook it in frustration. "Why won't you balance, you stupid thing?"

"Problems?" Rafe Malone's jovial voice jerked Zeke's head up.

He furrowed his forehead and glared at his friend.

Rafe leaned far too casually on the doorjamb, smirking in that upbeat way he did. Nothing fazed the man. In the thick of a gunfight, Rafe always remained as calm as a cucumber, cracking jokes while bullets pinged by. They all counted on his steadiness when they were in the thick of it, but his charm wore thin today.

"I hate accounting." Zeke eased back in his office chair and threw his pen on the desk. "I think trolls programmed QuickBooks."

Rafe laughed, rubbing his hand over his perfectly groomed red beard. "Accountants have to get their kicks somehow. If everyone mastered their diabolical program, then there wouldn't be any need for them."

Zeke chuckled, then lit up with a thought. "Hey, why don't you take a whack at it?"

"No way, man." Rafe held his hands out in front of him like he was warding off a wild dog or something. Zeke understood that—accounting was a beast. "You're not loading that on me."

"Come on. You know computers inside and out. Can hack into the highest level security systems. You're a wizard at this stuff."

"While I'm humbled that you acknowledge my general awesomeness and that I'm a Master of Technology, your flattery will not woo me to the dark side."

"You could have this done in no time flat." Zeke ran his hands through his hair as his frustration rose. "I've been here for hours, have looked at numbers until my eyes crossed, and still can't get the columns to balance."

"Dude, just admit it. We need to hire someone for all

of this." Rafe motioned with his hands at the chaotic office.

Zeke scowled as he glanced around at the papers overflowing the baskets, the sticky notes of various neon colors slapped onto the wall, and the general disorder of the room. He had hoped that setting up his security firm outside Glenwood Springs, Colorado would prove a brilliant idea. Just north of Aspen and west of Vail, located where all the rich and famous hung out, it had been a strategic move. It had proved better than any of them imagined. They'd been getting more calls than they could handle since the minute Rafe had designed their website and Zeke had contacted some acquaintances. While the influx of clients was excellent for the growing business, it'd left little time for mundane things like number crunching and office organization.

Zeke placed his elbows on the desk and rubbed his eyes with the heels of his hands. He didn't want to hire an outsider. His team was his family. He trusted them unconditionally. He couldn't imagine some stuffy office person melding with his men, but if he didn't do something soon, the business would suffer. They were already so busy he was putting the word out to other army friends to join them.

"You know I'm right, Cap," Rafe interrupted his thoughts. "We need help."

"Get out of here before the Good Idea Fairy suggests a certain cocky computer genius needs to do some organizing." Zeke lifted one eyebrow and motioned toward the piles of papers.

"Sir, yes sir." Rafe saluted with a smile and beat feet,

hollering to the house as he left. "Don't go near the Cap. He's liable to make you scrub toilets with a toothbrush or cut the grass with office scissors."

Zeke chucked the tennis ball he kept on his desk out the door. A thunk and an outraged cry of pain caused him to smile. The others in the living room ribbed Rafe, tempting Zeke to abandon the office and join them. A scowl replaced his smile as he glared at the mismatching numbers on the computer screen. His phone vibrated on the desk. Beatrice Thomas-soon-to-be-Bennett's picture smiled up at him from the screen.

He'd just met Beatrice a few weeks earlier when, by an unbelievable act of God, she had found herself on his friend's Chase's mountain. Zeke glanced at the two pictures hanging on the wall of his friends Hunter Bennett and Ethan Stryker. At least now he knew what had happened to Hunter, Zeke's best friend and army buddy who'd mysteriously disappeared a year and a half ago.

They had lost Ethan Stryker in a mission that had gone south just a few weeks before Hunter went on a camping trip and never returned. Instead of signing on for another tour like Zeke had planned, he had retired and moved here to help Hunter's brother Chase search. When nothing showed up after several weeks, Zeke decided to start Stryker Security Force and stick close to Chase. One by one, the other guys from Zeke's special forces team joined him when their turn came up for re-enlisting.

Over the last year and a half, he and Chase had spent countless hours searching the Rocky Mountains for any sign of Hunter. When Beatrice had arrived from the past with the rest of Hunter's story, the relief to know he hadn't died alone on the mountain had almost rocketed Zeke to the moon. The weight of not telling the others held him firmly on the earth. Chase and Beatrice had begged Zeke to keep her arrival on the down low. Though it tore at him to do so, he'd keep Hunter's story and Beatrice's jaunt forward through time to himself, hoping that as Beatrice got more comfortable in this time, especially after she married Chase, that he could convince them they could trust the rest of the team with the incredible story.

"Hey, Bea. You ready to leave Chase behind and run away with me into the sunset?" Zeke stood up from his chair and walked to the window.

The large, groomed yard butted up to an open field that extended all the way to the mountains. He'd bought the property just south of Glenwood for its enormous houses and acreage, where they had room to train and house clients securely if needed. Once a sprawling ranch, the property was perfect with its intimidating front gate and miles of barbed wire fencing.

Beatrice snorted, and Zeke could picture her cheeks pinking. "Zeke, you scoundrel. You know I'm madly in love with Chase and would never run off with you into the sunset or anywhere else."

"I'm hurt, Bea, truly hurt. Don't go easy on me or anything. Tell me how you really feel. I can take it." Zeke laced his voice with mock injury.

"You'll get over it." Her voice held a humor he was

glad to hear, especially after the turmoil she'd gone through.

"How's the planning going for the quickest wedding of the decade?" He shook his head, still in shock over the fact she and Chase were getting married the next day.

"That's why I'm calling. I need you to do me a favor."

"Chase getting cold feet? Need me to tie him down and hold him hostage until the ceremony?" Zeke knew that was a firm negative considering the way Chase was crazy over her.

"No, Chase isn't getting cold feet, and no, you don't have to tie him down."

"Hey!" Chase's exclamation came loud through the phone.

"I want Samantha and Evangeline to come to the wedding, but Sam doesn't think her car will make it up the mountain again in one piece. Do you think you can bring them with you?" Beatrice's request had him leaning against the desk in shock.

Zeke stifled a growl. Samantha had sauntered back into Chase's life because she needed something, mainly a father for her kid, and had nearly torn Beatrice and Chase apart. Their relationship had survived, and Beatrice had found a friendship with Samantha. Zeke wasn't sure about her, and it had taken every ounce of restraint he had not to have Rafe search her background. He didn't trust someone who would keep their child from the possible father for four years, no matter if she had good intentions or not.

"Yeah, I guess I can take her," he answered with a sigh.

"Thank you!" Beatrice gushed into the phone in a manner unlike the tough woman he admired. "I'm so happy. I'll send you her address and tell her you'll pick her up."

"Yeah, sure, that would be fine." He hung up the phone and turned back to the computer with a growl.

QuickBooks would have to wait for another day. He slammed the screen shut. He needed to pound his frustration out into the boxing bag. Better yet, Rafe obviously had plenty of time to spare. He grinned with menace as he hollered for Rafe and stomped out of the office.

SAMANTHA JONES RUSHED into the Canary Café, frantically putting her stuff in her cubby behind the counter. She was late—again. When her babysitter had called at the last minute and said she couldn't watch Sam's daughter, Evangeline, Samantha had called her minimal contacts trying to find someone else who could keep her daughter during her shift. She was so thankful Chase and Beatrice had said that they would take the little girl shopping with them while she went to work this afternoon. She couldn't afford to miss another shift.

She pulled on her apron and hurried out to see which zone she served. If anyone had told her two months before that she'd be living in a Colorado tourist town, serving quiche and lattes to be a bunch of upitty tourist, she would've laughed in their face.

Back in Texas, she'd had a stable job that provided well for her and Eva. Though most people would consider office work boring, she found it reliable and constant. That all changed when the Payne family decided they wanted Eva, even though their son Garrett had wanted nothing to do with her. She shuddered, thinking about the way they had forced her out of her job, hoping to drive her into their lives. Instead, she had run away, knowing the last thing she'd ever want for Eva was that manipulating family.

All she had now was aching feet, a tweaked back, and a near-empty bank account. She just prayed eventually she'd be able to find something better, something that gave them enough for more than the crappy apartment and beans and rice every night.

She pasted on a smile and walked over to her first table. "What can I get you today?"

After taking down the order, she went to the back and placed it into the system for the cook.

"Samantha!" George's barked shout startled her, making her jump. "You're late again. You mess up one more time and you're out of here."

"Sorry, George. I understand."

Samantha didn't blame him. She hadn't been a good employee. It surprised her George had kept her as long as he had, what with her having to miss shifts often because of lack of babysitters. She wasn't sure how she would make it, but she had to. She couldn't afford to move again.

"Don't listen to him," Cassidy said as she elbowed Samantha. "He's just grumpy today."

"I'd be grumpy too if I were him." Samantha exhaled and shrugged.

"Well, I know something that will make you happy."

Cassidy smiled slowly while wiggling her eyebrows down. "That handsome guy, Chai Latte with Coconut Milk is back."

Samantha rolled her eyes. Cassidy was funny like that, giving the regulars nicknames according to what they ordered most often. Samantha glanced out the window to the tables set up along the sidewalk. Sure enough, Chai Latte with Coconut Milk sat reading something on his phone, his forehead scrunched and mouth pinched.

Sam agreed with Cassidy that the man was good-looking. A woman would have to be blind not to notice the firm muscles in the too-tight shirt. His dark brown hair was cut short, framing his tanned and ridiculously handsome face. *Not in a million years.*

She turned back to inputting the order. Even if she was searching for love, Chai Latte had too much of a military vibe to be somebody she would even consider being interested in. Cassidy, on the other hand, seemed to be interested in every man walking through the café. She often left Sam chuckling as she swooned behind the counter, fanning herself dramatically every time a man walked by. Sam was glad she was over that stage in life. That's what being a starving single mom did to you— cancelled all your hormones so all you thought of was survival.

"Go ahead. I'm not interested."

"Come on." Cassidy pulled on Sam's arm. "It might just bring some sunshine into your day. He's always friendly."

Sam shook her head. "No, thank you. I have enough

sunshine in my life already. I don't want to add a guy to the mix. That's the last thing I should be doing. You go ahead, Cassidy." Sam motioned with her hands for Cassidy to go outside.

Cassidy wiggled her eyebrows and gave Sam a kissy face, then walked outside smiling big as Chai Latte with Coconut Milk looked up and grinned. Sam remembered when she used to be like Cassidy, carefree and fun, but that changed the day she became a mom. She wouldn't change being a mom for the world. She loved her baby girl, but some days were harder than others, especially with moving to an unfamiliar area.

She sighed, thankful that she had come to know Beatrice and had repaired her friendship with Chase. She never thought it would be possible, not with how she'd used him in college, killing their friendship in a moment of jealousy. At least one good thing had come out of being forced to leave Texas. She probably never would've contacted Chase if she hadn't been desperate. She shook away the thoughts and went back to work, knowing if George found her lollygagging, he'd fire her for sure. She wouldn't blame him if he did, but she'd do anything to keep Eva from having to sleep in the car again. She straightened her shoulders and placed the customers' drinks on her tray, determined to be the best employee George had ever had.

CHAPTER TWO

Zeke pulled up to the worn down apartment complex and double checked his navigation system to make sure he was in the right spot. He couldn't imagine anybody voluntarily staying in this dump, especially with a child. Paint was peeling off the exterior and a group of men hung around, loudly talking and drinking beers on the balcony of Samantha's floor even though it was only ten in the morning. The building looked like it used to be a motel that someone converted into apartments thirty years before from the style of the architecture and the outdoor balconies that led up to the different stories.

Zeke turned off his Bronco and got out of the truck, measuring up the men as he walked to the stairs. He climbed the steps and looked for Samantha's unit number. Finding it, he knocked loudly. From inside, he heard squealing moving closer to the door before it opened quickly to the most adorable little girl he'd ever seen. Bright blue eyes stared up at him from her light brown face. Freckles dotted her cheeks and nose like a hundred angels had kissed her. Her mouth dropped open as she ran her eyes up his length, and curly hair sprung out in all directions.

"Eva, I told you not to open the door." A woman rushed up, grabbing the girl and pulling the child behind her. "I'm sorry. Can I help you?" Her eyes widened before she dropped her gaze to the child peeking from behind her legs.

"I'm Zeke Greene. I'm here to pick you up."

"It's nice to meet you, Zeke. Sam ... Samantha Jones."

She extended her hand, and Zeke took it. It was small and soft in his large one. He cleared his throat. She was tiny, just like her hand. Not in a petite way, but skinny, like she didn't eat enough. Her face held strength as she stepped back, her cheeks sharp in her dark brown face.

"You probably should lock your door." Zeke hated that his voice came out rough, but he couldn't help it. This wasn't a neighborhood a gorgeous single woman with a cute kid should take chances in.

Samantha huffed and crossed her arms. "Yeah, well, I locked it. Eva must've jiggled it just right to pop it unlocked. It does that sometimes." Samantha held his stare. "Thank you for coming to pick us up. I really appreciate it."

"No problem." Don't be a jerk, Greene.

"Come on in. I just need to grab a couple more things and then we'll be ready." She waved him in and headed toward the back of the apartment as he stepped inside. "Make yourself comfortable."

She disappeared into the bedroom, and Zeke glanced around the apartment that held a threadbare brown couch, a small table with two chairs, a desk by the door, and a tiny kitchenette. He scowled. The place looked like it hadn't been remodeled since the 1970s with its puke green shag carpet and rust-colored paint. Nothing looked to be personal items except a few framed pictures on the table beside the couch.

"We need to hurry, or we're gonna be late," he called back to her as he pretended to not snoop.

"I'm sorry. I'll be quick, I promise." Samantha's voice came from the back of the apartment.

A tug at his hand drew his eyes down to a cherub face staring up at him.

"Those are pretty paintings on your arm, mister." Eva traced her finger along the tattoos that covered the back of his hand. "Do you have any more?"

"Yeah, sure." Zeke extended his other arm and pushed up his sleeve up to show her the tattoos inked on his forearm.

Eva smiled and giggled as she traced the flowers and birds that twined up and down his arm. Her eyes were wide as if it were a great secret that she had found. She grabbed his hand again and started swinging it back and forth. Her teeny hand disappeared completely into his. She looked healthy and happy, unlike her mom.

"Sorry about that." Samantha came from the back room carrying an outfit hanging inside of a garbage bag like a homemade garment bag, a rainbow backpack with a unicorn face on it, and a gym bag.

"Here, let me get that." He reached out and grabbed the makeshift garment bag.

"We get to see the horsies today," Eva chirped next to

him, giving his hand an extra tug during the swing. "I love horsies. My favorite is Storm, but Bea said I can't ride Storm yet."

Zeke's heart picked up a bit at the thought of the sweet little girl on that devil horse of Chase's. "I agree. I don't think that'd be a good idea."

Samantha grabbed her purse and opened the door. "Eva, let Mr. Greene's hand go, honey."

Eva didn't listen.

"It's just Zeke." He lifted Eva's hand high and wiggled it. "Come on, squirt. We have a wedding to go to."

Eva squealed and hugged his arm. Zeke chuckled, then sobered when he glanced at Samantha. Her pinched expression signaled her annoyance. Yeah, well, get in line, sister. He took the few steps to reach the balcony, lifting Eva with each step like a carnival ride. He turned just as Samantha pulled the door closed and locked it. She jiggled the handle before nodding and turning to follow.

"There's no deadbolt?" He liked this place less with every minute.

Samantha sighed. "No. The inside has a chain." She shrugged. "At night I push the desk in front of the door. Unfortunately, this is all I can afford right now."

They headed across the balcony toward the stairway. She stepped up even with them, and Eva grabbed her hand, lifting her legs up to swing between them. As they approached the stairs and the men that loitered outside the apartment there, Samantha tensed and Eva quieted, leaning into Zeke's side.

"Hey, sweet mama," one man yelled loud enough for the entire complex to hear.

Zeke hated men like this—men who would drink the day away, making trouble for others instead of getting off their butts and working. Just what did these guys do that let them hang around on a Monday morning? Whatever it was, Zeke didn't like Samantha and Eva living just a few doors down from that.

"The African queen's stepping out," another man chortled. "And look at that, she's planning on shacking up."

To her credit, Samantha held her head high and gazed forward, not acknowledging the comment. Her neck and cheeks darkened, and Zeke's blood ran hot. The stench of cigarettes and alcohol thickened, assaulting his nose.

"Come on, Queenie, I already told you I'd bow down at your feet. You don't have to go out with Muscles, there." The man reached out as Samantha passed and grabbed her arm. "I promise, you and me would have a pleasurable time."

She ripped her arm away and glared at the man, her hand clenching into a fist. Zeke pulled his hand free of Eva's and guided her and Samantha to the stairs. Once they were descending, he turned to the men. Taking one step toward the man who grabbed Samantha, Zeke invaded the jerk's space.

Zeke leaned in, making sure his voice pitched low and menacing, the voice he used to break countless terrorists during interrogations. "You touch her again, and you won't use your hand ... ever."

The man's eyes narrowed as Zeke stood up. He turned and headed down the stairs. Laughter followed him down. His mouth went dry at the ribbing going on behind him. He might have just made the situation worse for Samantha, though five minutes ago he wouldn't have thought it possible.

———

SAMANTHA TOOK a deep breath as she clicked Eva's car seat buckle and handed her a toy from her backpack. She closed the door, her face still hot with embarrassment and fear, and took another deep breath before climbing into the passenger seat. She still couldn't believe that Chai Latte with Coconut Milk turned out to be Beatrice's friend. She'd almost said something when she'd come out of the back of the apartment to find him standing there.

Zeke's smoky, earthy cologne that reminded her of fresh-cut grass on a summery day enveloped her. While she could protect herself and Eva if it came down to it, she was thankful that he had confronted those guys. She worried constantly about Eva's safety, especially in this sketchy complex.

She smiled hesitantly over at Zeke. "Sorry about that back there on the balcony."

"Do they do that often, bug you like that?" Zeke asked as he backed out of the parking space.

"Usually it's just a comment or two, but I just ignore them and walk by as fast as I can."

"Have you told your super about it?" He glanced over at her.

Samantha nodded. "Yeah, well, the super's that jerk's cousin. He wasn't concerned about it too much."

Zeke's hands tightened on the steering wheel as he pulled onto the interstate. She hated that she lived in such a dump, that Eva had to be around those types of men, but she didn't have a choice at this point. She was glad her lease was week to week, because as soon as she could afford to, she was finding a new place to rent.

"If you want, I can have one of my guys come by and fix your lock, make it sturdier. Maybe put a deadbolt in." Zeke's voice was hard with none of the smile she'd heard with Eva.

"Do you own a construction company or something?"

"No, I own a security firm. One of my guys is a master at all things mechanical and construction related." He drummed his thumb on the steering wheel.

Samantha suddenly wondered how he knew Chase. "So, have you known Chase and Beatrice long?"

"I have known Chase since he was in college. I was on his brother's Hunter's team with the army. I just met Beatrice a couple weeks ago." He still stared out the front window, not looking over at Samantha at all.

Her heart stuttered. She knew all about the military. Her father had been a soldier in the army. Though in reality, she never knew her father at all. He'd gotten himself killed in Iraq. Her mom had told her all about it, had warned her never to get involved with someone of that background—someone always chasing danger. She took her mom's advice to heart, saw how her mom struggled her entire life to get over the heartache.

Samantha realized when she moved out here that

even though Garrett's family was horrendous, it would be nice if Eva had a father, someone that Samantha could share the load with. She never considered marrying Chase, but the hope that he might be Eva's father instead of Garrett had galvanized her to push past her embarrassment and approach him with the possibility. It would have made things so much easier for Samantha if Chase had been Eva's father. She wouldn't have to worry about the Payne family and what they might do next if they found her. But that hope died when Chase's paternity test came back negative. The results hadn't surprised her. Nothing in her life was ever easy.

"So, you were in the military with Hunter? Why did you get out?" Samantha cringed at her question. She had no business asking him something so personal.

He shrugged. "It was time."

Yep, she shouldn't have asked that question. She wondered if he was always this gruff or if it was just with her. He seemed so friendly when he came into the Canary Café, smiling up at Cassidy when she came to take his order. Sure, he looked tough and could probably follow through with his threat he gave the man on the balcony, but he'd never come across as harsh.

"How long have you been in business?"

"Not too long, about six months."

"Everything's going okay?"

"Yeah."

Hookay. Just shut your mouth. Obviously, Zeke didn't want to talk about it. That was okay. She really didn't want to know his business, anyway. She'd always kept her distance from people in the military and law enforcement, her mom's warnings ringing in her ear. She took a deep breath and looked out the window, deciding that she would watch the scenery go by instead of finishing this torturous conversation.

"So, Beatrice tells me you are a waitress."

Samantha turned to him with wide eyes, surprised he'd decided to talk to her. "Yeah, for now anyway. I work over at the Canary Café."

"I like the Canary Café. They make pretty good food." Zeke's voice held excitement for the first time since he started talking to her.

Samantha turned to him with a smile. "And they make a fantastic chai latte with coconut milk, too."

Zeke looked over at her, his eyebrows winging up toward his hairline. Her smile got bigger, and her heart beat faster in the chest. Yes, Zeke was dangerous with his handsome looks and his killer brown eyes, but she had to remember that she wasn't interested in guys right now. She had enough on her plate. She didn't want any man, especially one with the job he had.

"How did you know that?"

"Cassidy names all of her favorite customers by what they order a lot, especially, if they're good-looking guys." Samantha looked forward through the windshield, heat rising up her neck. Now why'd she have to say he was good looking? "She has a little bit of a crush on you."

Zeke groaned and rubbed his hand over his short, dark brown hair. "Oh, great. I didn't think I'd done anything to encourage her."

"Oh, you didn't." Samantha turned to him with a

chuckle. "You're nothing special. Cassidy has crushes on all the hot guys that come in."

Samantha's eyes widened as he turned to her and cocked an eyebrow. She cringed and tried to smile a little bigger.

"Mr. Zeke is special, Mama. He has pretty drawings all up and down his arms." Eva's singsong voice floated forward from the back. "And he protected you from the mean man."

Samantha turned around in her seat and looked back at Eva with a smile. "Mr. Zeke is a friendly guy, Eva. I didn't mean it when I said he wasn't special."

Samantha turned forward and gave him another brief smile. Maybe she shouldn't avoid men like they were the plague. She never had so much trouble talking to them before, but since Garrett crushed her heart and left her pregnant, she had been a little gun-shy around them. She'd figured it was better to steer clear completely than risk taking a chance at love again.

"Do you think I'll be able to ride the horse today, Mama?" Eva asked as she kicked her feet against the back of Samantha's seat.

"I don't think so, honey. We're going up for Beatrice and Chase's wedding. There won't be enough time to ride the horses today." Samantha turned around in her seat again. "Could you please stop knocking the back of my seat?"

"But can I at least see the horsies?" Eva's pleading tone grated down Samantha's spine. She loved her daughter, but sometimes she hated the whining voices that a four-year-old could make.

"Hey, squirt. I'll take you to see the horses after the wedding, okay?" Zeke smiled at Eva in the rearview mirror.

Samantha clutched her hand around the door handle, trying not to get upset at Zeke's interference. She knew he was only helping, but him telling Eva that he would take her to see the horses hurt, made her feel like she wasn't being a good mom. She knew it was irrational. He had suggested nothing of the sort. Maybe she was just touchy on the subject, but she always had to be on—always had to be ready for when the next person said something about her parenting skills. She'd gotten attacked enough the last few months from the Payne family that she knew exactly how that felt.

Samantha continued to look out the window, watching the scenery change from sagebrush to aspen trees dressed in golden leaves. The farther they drove the winding road, climbing up into the mountains, the looser her shoulders got. She let Eva talk Zeke's ear off, pretending not to listen. She refused to allow the low rumble of his voice and the soft way that he spoke to her daughter to cause her heart to skip a beat.

CHAPTER THREE

Zeke tried to ignore Chase as he paced back and forth, waiting for Beatrice to come down from the house. He tried to keep his mind off the conversation in the car with Samantha. Try being the key word, but failing. What was it about her that drew him in like a moth to a flame?

He shook his head as the screen door opened and out came Eva, yelling and screaming that Beatrice was coming. Zeke chuckled. That girl sure had some spunk. He looked up as Samantha came out the door and straightened. She had changed from her T-shirt and jeans into a purple-colored sundress that made her skin glow. It flowed over her body and landed just above her knees.

Zeke swallowed and forced his heartbeat to slow. There was no way he wanted to get into a relationship again, especially not one that involved kids. He'd had his share of that with his ex-fiancée, Gillian. She'd grabbed his heart and ripped it right out of his chest when she'd taken her little girl and left, moving on to someone who could provide for them better. He wondered if she would've stayed if she had known he'd be inheriting billions in a few years. He glared, upset that Samantha had kicked up memories he'd buried deep long ago.

It wasn't like he had anything to worry about anyway, Zeke reminded himself. According to Samantha, he was nothing special. He clenched his jaw at the memory of her saying that. Sure, she had called him hot, but following it with how special he wasn't really checked his ego. He hated that it bothered him so much and didn't quite understand why. The ceremony finished before Zeke could focus and pay attention, and he was determined to push the contrary woman out of his head.

"Kind of cranky today, man?" Chase walked up to him. "What's eating you?"

"Nothing much," Zeke said, determined to get out of this funk so he didn't ruin his close friend's wedding. "Just thinking about work and how much of a mess I have at home."

"What do you mean? Are your jobs not going well?" Chase moved toward the barbecue grill that was emitting a smell that tortured Zeke's hungry stomach.

"No, it's not a client. I'm bogged down right now with paperwork, accounting mainly, but everything else too." Zeke peeked over Chase's shoulder into the grill filled with ribs, and his stomach growled.

Chase chuckled and raised his eyebrows. "You hungry?"

"Starving, man."

"You know, Samantha went to college for marketing and accounting." Chase glanced over at Zeke. "You could always hire her to help you out."

That was the last thing Zeke wanted. He didn't need her around all the time with her swirly skirt and her big brown eyes always gazing at him. Not that she gazed at him. In fact, she'd practically ignored him the entire ride up. But her soft citrus smell had teased him when she got into the car. He knew having her in the office would be more than he wanted to deal with at this point.

"I'll keep that in mind." Zeke took a drink of his soda to give him some time to change the conversation. "So where are you off to on your honeymoon?"

"We're heading to Fiji. Beatrice has never been anywhere tropical, so I thought I would take her to a resort on one of the islands."

"That'll be nice." Zeke had to admit he was a little jealous of Chase. Beatrice was amazing, even with her history. He couldn't never imagine going through everything that she'd gone through and still being as strong as she was.

Eva ran up and threaded her fingers through Zeke's large ones. She swung them back and forth, smiling up at him. Chase looked down and back up, his eyebrow cocking and a little smirk tweaking his mouth. Zeke glared at him before turning a smile down on Eva.

"Mr. Zeke, can we go see the horsies now?" Eva smiled prettily and used both her hands to cup his in a pleading motion.

Zeke paused for a second, looked up into the sky, and put his finger on his chin like he was thinking hard. He then looked back and forth and bent down to be on her level.

"Do you think it's a good time to go see the horses

now? It's almost time to eat." Zeke forced doubt into his voice.

Eva brought his hand up to her face and squeezed it between hers. She nodded, jumping on her toes like she could hardly contain her excitement.

"All right, then I guess it's time to go see the horses, but it'll have to be a quick trip. Then after lunch, we'll go visit for longer." Zeke squeezed her hand.

Eva squealed, jumping into his arms and almost toppling him over. He caught himself and gave her a pat on the back. He looked up just in time to see Chase's hand covering his smile.

He cleared his throat. "But first, young lady, go change back into your jeans. You don't want to get your pretty flower dress all dirty."

Eva gave him another squeeze around the neck then took off for the house, slamming the sliding door as she went inside. Zeke stood up as Chase burst out laughing.

"There a problem?"

"No, man." Chase rubbed his hand over his mouth. "I'm just wondering how long it took her to wrap you around her little finger."

"It's not that." He shrugged and leaned against the awning post. "She just was so excited about seeing the horses, I didn't want to let her down."

"Sure. I understand that." He smiled and flipped the ribs. Chase's smile fell as he turned back to Zeke. "I'm a little worried about Sam, actually. Beatrice said something about somebody forcing Sam to leave her old home. I don't know what it's all about, but it's kinda got me worried. With us leaving, she really doesn't have anybody else around to help her out if she needs it. Would you mind keeping an eye on her for me?"

Zeke inwardly groaned. He didn't want to be keeping an eye on her for himself or anyone else. She'd already consumed too much of his brain space in the little time that he knew her. He also knew that he wouldn't stop worrying about her, given her current living conditions.

"Yeah, sure. You almost done burning those things or what?" Zeke motioned toward the grill with his soda can.

Chase looked at him in mock indignation. "I'll have you know these are gonna be the best ribs you've ever had." He opened the lid and started transferring the meat onto the tray. "Make yourself useful, and go tell Beatrice the food's done."

Zeke saluted Chase and purposely bumped into him as he walked past. Chase's yell as he fumbled with the tray brought a satisfied grin to Zeke's mouth. The grin fell as he stepped through the door and saw Samantha standing with Beatrice. Her mouth was stretched into a beautiful smile that kicked Zeke's heart rate up a beat. This was not good. There is no way he would allow himself to get distracted, especially not by someone like Samantha Jones.

SAMANTHA LOOKED around the café to make sure that her tables had everything they needed and breathed a sigh of relief. The last few days had gone better than she could've imagined, but that was probably because of Eva still being excited about seeing the horses two days earlier. She smiled at the thought of Zeke holding Eva up against the corral as her daughter fed apples to the horses.

Her little girl's giggling had filled Samantha with a warmth and weightlessness that she hadn't felt in a very long time. It had taken her almost the entire rest of their visit with Chase and Beatrice, and the ride home, to realize the feeling was euphoric and without fear. After months of being on edge and stressed, worried the Paynes were just around the corner waiting to pounce, those few hours of peacefulness had left her limbs loose and her mind drowsy. Of course, that changed the minute she closed her apartment door and the yelling of the neighbors leached through the walls.

Samantha shook her head and grabbed a tray to clear off the table. She'd been spending far too much time thinking about Zeke and his interactions with Eva. Far too much time wondering how it'd feel with his arms wrapped around her like they had around Eva. She fanned her shirt and mentally scolded herself. Again. For the thousandth time. She couldn't afford to have him invade her mind at work and have George fire her for lollygagging.

She turned around with the tray and froze. Zeke walked through the door in all his glory, his muscles pulling his shirt taut as he moved. So much for keeping her mind off of a certain man. He pointed to a tall table with stools next to the window and waved her over. She nodded, wishing George had told *her* to organize the storage room instead of Cassidy. She felt like Dory from *Finding Nemo* as she repeated, "Just act normal. Just act normal," in her head. His intoxicating, earthy scent assaulted her senses and made her knees weak the instant she stepped close. She hugged the tray to her chest to gird herself.

She forced a smile. "Hey, Chai Latte with Coconut Milk. What can I get you?"

Zeke chuckled, the sound low and entirely too delicious. "How about a chai latte with coconut milk?"

"That's new. Anything el—"

The vibration of her phone buzzed in her pocket and the nursery rhyme she'd set as Eva's school's ringtone sang about monkeys. She shoved the tray at Zeke and fumbled for the phone. Images of Eva breaking her arm or choking on a grape flashed through her mind. Her hands shook so much as she pulled it out of her pocket, she could hardly tap the green answer circle.

"Hello? This is Samantha."

"Samantha, hey, it's Patti." Eva's teacher's normally chirpy voice was tense. "So, we had a situation here I thought you should know about."

Samantha clung to her forearm that held her phone up to her ear, pulling her arms tight against her. "What happened? Is Eva all right?"

Zeke's eyebrows furrowed, and he set the tray on the table. He placed his hand on her arm. The contact calmed her enough so she could think clearly.

"Eva's fine." Patti's words had Sam's breath whooshing from her. "It's just that someone showed up here and tried to take Eva."

"Someone tried to kidnap Eva?" Samantha's knees buckled. She would've collapsed to the floor if it hadn't been for Zeke pulling a chair out and pushing her in it. The Paynes had found her.

"No, not really. Well, I guess you could say that," Patti's voice prattled on.

"Patti, what happened?"

"Well, a woman came and said she was Eva's aunt, and that she wanted to take Eva out for a treat."

Sam stared at Zeke with wide eyes as her heart threatened to pound out of her chest. "You didn't let her—"

"No, no. Eva's still here. We told the lady that without parental consent, we didn't let children leave with others."

"I'm coming to get her." She stood and bumped into Zeke, who backed up quickly.

Ending the call, she snatched up the tray and marched to the kitchen. "George, I have to leave. There's been an issue at Eva's school."

"Is she okay?" George asked, crossing his arms across his chest.

"Yeah, she's fine."

"Then you can't go." George leaned against the prep counter.

"What do you mean I can't go?" Sam tried to stop the rise in her voice.

"I meant what I said, Samantha. One more problem and you're fired." George's jaw clenched. "If you leave, then I have to spend the next hour trying to find someone to cover your shift. I need someone I can depend on."

Samantha's mind reeled. She needed this job, but someone had just tried to take her daughter. It had taken her so long to find this position; would she even be able to find another? What if whoever had gone by the school tried to do something else before she got there?

Her shoulders slumped. "I understand. I'm sorry I've been such a hassle for you."

George sighed and uncrossed his arms. "You're an excellent worker, Sam. I just need someone I can rely on."

Sam nodded. Her throat felt like sandpaper, and tears blurred her vision. She pushed through the door and startled when she practically ran into Zeke. Blinking rapidly to clear the moisture from her eyes, she moved around him and grabbed her stuff.

"I'll follow you over, if that's okay?" Zeke pulled his keys from his pocket.

Samantha nodded, not caring why he wanted to come. He led the way out of the café, scanning the area as they approached her vehicle. She pulled up short when she noticed his Bronco parked next to hers. He opened her car door and shot a look of concern her way. She skirted around him and got in, rolling the window down as he closed the door.

"What's the name of her school just in case we get separated?" Zeke leaned on the open window.

"Sunny Day—" Samantha turned the key and a clicking noise met her ears.

She looked across the gauges and tried again. No rattling and coughing like the car was struggling to breathe sounded, just an ominous clicking followed by silence. She leaned her head on the steering wheel, willing herself not to flip out and break down to a blubbering mess.

"Come on." Zeke's whisper and soft touch across her back almost broke the dam loose. "I'll drive you there."

She peered up into his dark, brown eyes that held such understanding and nodded, letting him open the car door for her. She got into Zeke's Bronco in a daze.

She was glad for the momentary reprieve, for a chance to catch her breath. Maybe by then she could pull herself together and come up with some kind of plan to keep her daughter safe and not have them living on the streets. Or maybe everyone was right, and she really couldn't be the mom Eva needed. She closed her eyes and leaned her head against Zeke's passenger door, hollowed out to her very core.

CHAPTER FOUR

Frustration welled in Zeke's gut as he made his way to Eva's school. Everything in him wanted to push the pedal down and speed through town to get to her, but he knew getting pulled over would not help the situation at all. He glanced over at Samantha where her head laid against the passenger window. Her eyes were closed, her jaw clenched. Her strength impressed him. That she hadn't broken down in tears or railed at her boss surprised him. Her boss's words as he fired her still rang in Zeke's ears.

"So, what is going on here, Samantha?" Maybe if he could get her talking, he could figure out how to fix this problem.

Samantha sighed so deeply he thought it came all the way from her toes and lifted her head as if it weighed a hundred pounds. She looked over at him. "Patti, Eva's teacher, called to say that someone tried to come and pick up Eva. She said the woman claimed she was Eva's family."

"Do you know who it could've been?" Zeke pulled to a stop at the light and looked over at her.

Samantha rubbed her hand across her forehead. "Well, the only aunt Eva has is her Aunt Kiki, Garrett's sister."

"Would she do something like this?"

"I don't know, maybe. I mean, she always seemed nice, and I can't imagine her doing something like that, but with everything that happened with Garrett's family the last few months ... it's just ... I don't know. I wouldn't put anything past them at this point."

"What do you mean, everything that happened with them?" The light turned green. Zeke pressed on the gas and continued on to the school.

"A few months ago Garrett's family started contacting me with threats that they would take me to court for custody of Eva. I hadn't heard from Garrett for months before Eva was born, didn't even realize they knew, so their interest in her came as a surprise." Samantha looked out the window and twisted her hands. "I guess Garrett died in a car accident a few years ago. Our relationship wasn't the healthiest, especially during the end. So when he wanted nothing to do with Eva, I figured it was a blessing in disguise. I wouldn't have to worry about him and his family and what they'd teach her. But ... his parents somehow found out that Eva was his, and they kind of became obsessed."

"What kind of things have they done?" Zeke's heart rate increased with the magnitude of the situation.

"They were never civil. Started right away about how I was unfit to raise their granddaughter, and they would get custody of Eva. I told them they wouldn't succeed, that the court system would never let that happen." Samantha looked over at him. "After that, things started getting crazy."

"Crazy how?"

"I don't know, I guess ... I maybe started getting a little paranoid, but it felt like people were always watching us. And then the Paynes put pressure on my boss to fire me."

"They had you fired? How did they do that?" Zeke was not liking this family, and, if what Samantha said was true, she and Eva were in serious trouble.

"I'm not sure what they did, but the next thing I know, I'm getting fired. My boss told me he didn't need to put up with the pressure he was getting about me. The next day, the Paynes invited me and Eva to move in with them. It was all so weird and scary, quite scary." Her sentence trailed off to a whisper. She cleared her throat. "So instead of moving in with them, I ran away, and we disappeared. I didn't know where to go. I knew through friends that Chase had moved here to Colorado, so I just kind of ended up here."

Zeke could tell in her tone that she was leaving something out. "Do you think they could've found you?"

"Probably. I don't know. It's not like I knew how to hide where I was going. I've done nothing like this before. Never had to." Samantha grabbed her purse and fiddled with the handle. "I don't know what I will do now."

The last words were so quiet he almost missed them. When he told Chase that he would think about hiring Samantha, he never actually thought he would. In fact, at the time, he wanted to keep her far from his thoughts. But his mind had circled back to her throughout the last few days. If she could help him get his office straightened out, why not hire her? Just because he kept wondering if her skin was as smooth as it looked, and the worry about her and Eva's safety had kept him up late at night, didn't mean he had to rush in and sweep them up onto his stallion and ride off into the sunset. He knew from experience not all women wanted to be saved. She sighed heavily again next to him, and he knew he couldn't hold off asking her any longer.

Zeke cleared his throat. "I came into the café today to talk to you about something." She turned her hazel eyes to him and cocked her eyebrow. "The thing is, Chase said something about you going to college for accounting and marketing. Is that right?"

"Yeah, he's right. I did the accounting and marketing for a law firm in Texas for the last three years." Her eyes sparked with interest for the first time since he met her.

"I've been trying to figure out accounting and managing the office, but I have just been so busy with clients, and honestly, I hate it. You think you might want to give it a go?"

Samantha's forehead crinkled, and she looked at him. "Give it a go? What would that look like?"

Zeke ran his hand across the back of his neck and shrugged. "I don't know exactly. I have a massive pile of receipts. I've tried to set up QuickBooks, but everything is just chaos. I need somebody to come in and organize and get us all straightened out. Is that something you could do?"

"So would this be a permanent job or would it just be something temporary?" Hesitation had returned to her voice.

"Well, it would depend on what you want to do. If you want to just come in and set things up, we could do that. If you want the job on a more permanent status, if we all mesh, you could do that, too." Why did the thought of the job only being temporary clench his gut?

"Why would you do this? Why would you help me? You don't even know me, don't really like me?"

Zeke snapped his head to her. "I never said I didn't like you."

She scoffed. "You smile at everyone but me. Every conversation we've had you spoke in gruff tones."

She crossed her arms over her chest like she needed protection. From him. He'd been such a jerk.

"I'm sorry if that's how I've treated you. I didn't mean to be rude." True, but Zeke also knew he hadn't meant to be overly nice, either. "Listen Samantha, I need your help. Any of my guys will tell you I've been yelling at the computer for the last two weeks, trying to get it to work. I guess it just worked out that you needed a job at the same time I needed an accountant."

He pulled into the parking lot of the daycare and took the keys out of the ignition. He turned to her as she stared out the front window, wringing her hands. She clenched her jaw and pulled her shoulders back like she was steeling herself for combat. She was beautiful.

"Okay, I'll take you up on your offer. Can I start tomorrow?"

"That would work out just fine. Let's go get Eva and get you home."

Zeke went into the daycare with Samantha and listened to Eva's teacher describe the woman who had come in. Samantha was sure that it had been Garrett's sister Kiki from the description. That someone would come to try to take the girl from school worried Zeke. He got them into the Bronco and took them back to her apartment.

"Mind if I come up and check things out real fast?" Zeke asked, not wanting to intrude, though the desire to protect them burned within his chest.

"I'm not opposed to that." She gave him a small smile before turning her gaze upstairs.

Zeke was glad that no men were hanging out on the balcony today. He wasn't sure if his current mindset would handle another confrontation well. She got to the door and reached to unlock it. It pushed open with barely a touch.

All of Zeke's senses fired, alert as he pushed Samantha and Eva behind him. He glanced into the apartment but saw no movement.

He turned to Samantha and focused intently on her eyes. "I want you to follow me in. I don't want you to wait out here. Stay close behind me. If anything happens, you run. Got it?"

She gave a small nod as her eyes widened, and she pulled Eva into her arms. He handed her his keys and pulled his gun from his concealed holster. Giving Samantha one last, hard look, he eased into her apartment. He scanned the tiny room, searching for anything out of the ordinary. Everything appeared untouched. He slinked toward the back. One of Samantha's small hands fisted into the back of his shirt.

Before he entered the bedroom, he glanced back. Samantha turned to look at him as she surveyed the room. He mouthed, "Okay?" She nodded once and adjusted the grip on his shirt. He slowly pushed open the door to the bedroom, scanning the area for any intruders. The bare room was empty. He signaled to Samantha to wait and crossed to the closet. Taking a deep breath, he pushed the closet door open and surveyed the tight space. Empty.

With a grunt, he turned to Samantha and Eva and holstered his gun. "Pack up your stuff. You're coming with me."

"Wait, what? What do you mean, coming with you?" Samantha questioned, tightening her arms around Eva.

"Samantha, you can stay here if you want, but it's not safe for you and Eva anymore. I have an apartment above my garage that's empty at the moment. You and Eva can live there if you want. Part of the benefits of your new job."

Indecision played across her face. He curled his toes in his shoes so he didn't do something to make her choose to stay. She met his gaze and nodded once.

Zeke grabbed the gym bag she'd taken to the wedding from the closet and tossed it to her. He then snatched the suitcase from the top shelf in the closet. Laying it on the bed, he opened it and started piling their clothes in.

CHAPTER FIVE

Samantha's hands shook, so she crossed her arms and shoved them under her armpits. Glenwood whizzed by as Zeke drove them to his house. Which was now her home. She shook her head. If her heart wasn't still racing in her throat, she might have put up more of an argument. She peeked over at Zeke, whose hands strangled the steering wheel, his cheek muscles clenched tight. Maybe she should have.

She looked back out the windshield and squeezed her arms around her. She had almost changed her mind. Had a good argument worked up in her head as she had marched into the living room and placed Eva on the couch. She hadn't wanted her baby girl in the middle of what she knew would be a fight.

When she had turned to stomp back to the bedroom and give Zeke the what for, a scent had slipped into her nose and froze her feet. It had been faint, and she hadn't noticed it when she stayed glued to Zeke's back, waiting for the instant he told her to run. Then, she hadn't been able to smell anything but her own fear and Zeke's earthy scent. But standing in the living room, her indignation had leached out with the faint scent of the expensive cologne Garrett had always doused himself in. Someone from the Payne family had been in her apartment. A shiver slid like ice down her shirt, and she focused on the scenery as it passed.

She blinked and wondered when the city had given way to country. There were few houses now, and the few places she could see were situated far from each other. The car slowed, and Zeke pulled into a drive. Her insides quivered as they pulled under the massive archway with Silver Wolf Ranch twisted in iron and an iron wolf howling to the sky. She shot a look at Zeke, who stared forward through the windshield. When she looked back forward, a gasp clogged in her throat.

"Mr. Zeke, you live in a castle?" Eva's amazed voice mirrored Samantha's thoughts as they drove up the drive.

Fields, turned brown with the cool fall air, bordered both sides of the drive up to the house. Not a house ... a mansion, Samantha corrected herself. The enormous log structure looked out over the Colorado Mountains that jutted up on all sides of the valley. It sat up on a hill that slightly declined down to a golden aspen forest like a regal sentry keeping guard. She figured that was an appropriate description of Zeke keeping guard.

The closer they got, the quicker her heart beat in her chest. This wasn't like any house she had ever seen. It was tall, at least two stories high, and completely made of log. She imagined the green roof would blend in with the surroundings when it was summer, but with the autumn browns and oranges, it was a stark contrast. The drive circled up, and she noticed a sizeable building that looked like stables on one side of the circle drive, a gigantic four-car garage, and another house down a little drive that shot off toward the left. The house off to the side was almost just as big as the house on the primary drive. Zeke pulled up to a garage door attached to the main house and turned off the Bronco. She wasn't sure how she would feel comfortable in a place as fancy as this.

She turned her wide eyes to Zeke and pointed to the house. "You live here?"

"Yeah. When I started up Stryker Security Force, I wanted to have a place that we could set up operations and house clients that needed to lie low."

"How in the world did you afford all of this?" Samantha slapped her hand over her mouth and shook her head. "I'm sorry. That was rude. You don't have to answer me."

Zeke smirked as he cocked one of his eyebrows. "When the boys and I were overseas, we kind of stumbled into some money." He motioned quotes with his fingers when he said stumbled.

Samantha narrowed her eyes. She didn't know exactly what he meant, but her imagination started running wild. Zeke burst out laughing and pointed at her.

"You should see your face right now." Zeke hit his hand on the steering wheel. "I'm just kidding. It wasn't anything like that. My grandpa died, and he hated my dad, so he left me all his money. It gave me the opportunity to start this the way I wanted to." Zeke shrugged, wiped beneath his eyes with his finger, and open the car door. "Let's go see who's around."

Samantha fumbled with the door handle and grabbed her purse. As she stepped out of the car, her gaze traveled the height of the house. Her mouth gaped open again. She shook her head and turned to get Eva out of the back of the car. To her surprise, Zeke already had Eva out and had her in his arms, tickling her to get her to laugh.

"Are you ready to meet the guys, squirt? You gotta go easy on them. They're a bit delicate." Zeke smiled at Eva.

She hugged Zeke around the neck and then pushed back, putting her hands on both of his cheeks. Samantha chuckled as Eva's face transformed into her serious expression. Samantha's hands became sweaty with the thought of what her daughter was about to ask.

"Mr. Zeke, are you a prince or something? You live in a house like a prince. Are you like one of those guys in my princess movies I watch?" Eva's eyebrows furrowed as she tried to figure it out.

Zeke burst out laughing, his head falling back in merriment. Samantha had never seen anyone as handsome as he was at that moment. The joyful sound that rushed out of him hit her like an anvil and almost caused her to stumble back. Working and living here was not a good idea, not a good idea at all.

"Nope, squirt, I'm not a prince. Just a man trying to take care of his family." Zeke looked up and smiled over at Samantha. "Come on, let's go meet the guys."

Samantha stumbled over her feet as she tried to keep up with Zeke. She looked out over the land as she climbed the stairs to the front door and sucked in a breath, almost choking on her spit.

"You have a lake?" Shock was thick in Samantha's voice.

"Nah, it's just a pond. The creek feeds into it, and we stock it with fish. So, there's lots of land here, little squirt. I don't want you running off to where we can't see you, okay?" Zeke looked at Eva, and she nodded. "Now that building used to be the stables, but we converted it into storage, a shooting range, and gym. If you like working out or you want to shoot some guns, that's where you can do that."

Samantha felt a little warm with the thought of holding any kind of weapon in her hand. She shook her head. "I probably won't be using the shooting range. I'm not too fond of guns. Thank you, though."

Zeke shrugged, then pointed to the house off to the side. "That house down the other drive is where most of the guys live. In the garage next to the stables is where you'll be living. There's an apartment on the second floor."

Samantha nodded when he looked at her. With her mouth as dry as it was, she wasn't sure if she could talk. He headed the rest of the way up the stairs and opened the door. The sound of loud shouting and good-natured arguing filled the air, making Samantha's steps slow.

As she entered the house, Samantha could hardly believe the chaos. Men, large like Zeke, were playing some kind of video game in the living room, yelling at the screen and each other. She stepped in and marveled at the large open room. She'd never seen anything like it with its crisscrossing beams, rock fireplace that claimed the entire wall, and dead animals looking down at her. Windows completely lined the far wall, looking out over the meadow and the pond. The mountains jutted up in the distance, and she had seen nothing as beautiful as what lay before her. She'd seen a lot of marvelous houses in her time, but nothing that compared to the way this place balanced grandeur with hominess.

A spicy smell filled the air and had her stomach growling so loud she was glad the noise from the men covered it. Zeke turned around and glared at her stomach before turning back to the room. How embarrassing. Not only did he have to see her pitiful lack of food in their apartment when he'd helped her pack up, but now her stomach was protesting like she hadn't fed it in weeks. Which she hadn't. Not really. She pressed a hand to her belly and commanded it to keep quiet.

"Shut it!" Zeke hollered into the chaos.

Samantha flinched. The silence that fell in the house was instant. She shrank as three sets of eyes turned to them.

"Guys, I'd like you to meet someone." Zeke walked into the room. "This little squirt here is Eva." Zeke tickled Eva in the belly and made her giggle.

"Hi." Eva waved and smiled at the guys.

"And this is her mom, Samantha. Samantha will be our accountant and office manager. They'll be moving into the apartment above the garage." Zeke motioned to her.

"Hallelujah! Praise the Lord!" A man with perfectly styled auburn hair and a full beard raised his hands as if in a revival. "You've finally buckled and followed my superior advice and got help."

Zeke glared at the man, and a projectile flew across the room, hitting the bearded man in the head. Eva giggled, and Samantha smiled.

"Sosimo, man, watch the hair!" The man ran his hand over his still perfect hair.

"Knock it off, Rafe. We don't want to give Samantha the wrong impression right off the bat." A good-looking black man approached them.

He was tall like Zeke, with lean muscles attempting to escape his cowboy shirt with pearl snap buttons down the front. He wore boot cut pants and black cowboy boots that were contrary to his large frame that would put Dwayne Johnson to shame.

She quickly scanned the others in the room and realized they were all fit beyond belief and gorgeous. Just great. She'd landed in a grown-up version of a frat house. She tightened her grip on her purse and tried to swallow, but her mouth was a desert. She couldn't do this. She forced a smile as the man approached.

"Hi. I'm Derrick Nicholson." He shook her hand, then turned toward the group. "Sosimo is in the kitchen making dinner."

A Latin man waved at her as he stirred something on the stove. She squinted. She'd never seen a stove made of copper before.

"Do you cook?" Derrick asked, turning her attention back to him. "Because it'd be great if we could plug you into the rotation, bring a little variety to the table."

Though they hadn't been able to buy many groceries lately, she had always loved to cook and bake. With her mother's long hours at the hospital while Samantha grew up, she had taken over the cooking. She'd always tried to ease her mom's workload.

She nodded. "Yeah, I can cook."

Zeke growled. "Derrick, we aren't forcing her to cook."

"I don't mind, really. I'd love to be put on the rotation."

Rafe bounded up and pulled her into a bear hug, picking her up off her feet and turning her around before setting her down. She tried to steady herself on her wobbly knees. Derrick rolled his eyes and threw up his hands as he turned to Zeke. Sosimo's face split into a smile. Zeke scowled, his eyebrows so low she wondered if he could see.

"I'm so glad you're going to bail Zeke out. He's been a bear the last few weeks trying to figure all that out." Rafe stepped back and threw his arms wide. "Welcome to the Marvelous MAN-sion, where all your manly dreams come true."

The men groaned. Samantha smirked at his emphasis on the man part of the word. Though it surprised her, Rafe's joking loosened the band around her chest.

"Dude, I thought I told you to stop calling it that." Zeke set Eva down. "Try to act your age, just once ... please."

"What would be the fun in that?" Rafe bent down in front of Eva and turned her this way and that, searching her for something.

"Rafe, what are you doing?" Zeke ground out through clenched teeth.

"Zeke, you didn't tell us you were bringing home a fairy princess." Rafe's words had Eva giggling. "If I find her wings, she has to give me a wish."

Eva covered her laughing mouth with her tiny fingers.

"What do you think, Princess Eva? Are you going to let Ol' Rafe see your wings?" Rafe put his hands on his hips.

Eva shook her head, her eyes sparkling with delight.

"No?" Rafe slumped dramatically, then brightened back up. "I guess I just need to show you my loyalty." Rafe scooped her up, and she threw her arms around his neck in an enormous hug. "Come, my lady, let's see what your chef Sos is preparing for your enjoyment."

Zeke touched Samantha's elbow, shooting lightning up her arm and sending butterflies to riot in her belly. It wasn't a pleasurable feeling on an empty stomach. She didn't want lightning and butterflies, period. Zeke stuffed his hands in his pockets.

"While Sos is finishing up dinner, why don't I show you your place?" He tilted his head back out the door and started walking.

Samantha glanced to where Eva sat on the counter entertaining Rafe and Sosimo. She hesitated. The thought of leaving Eva with a group of rowdy men left her fingers itching to snatch her back. They all laughed at something Eva said, and her smile grew larger.

"She'll be all right, I promise. They may seem rough and rowdy, but they'd all do anything to keep her safe ... anything." Zeke's soft words made her jump. She turned to him and nodded. "Come on. Let me show you your new digs."

He walked out the door. Sam took one last look at Eva and turned to follow Zeke. She tried to keep her mouth from gaping as the rustic opulence hit her anew. A rock fountain flowed in the middle of the large circle drive. She wasn't sure how she'd missed the thing, but the way it blended with the surroundings instead of stuck out had her admiring the ingenuity of the design. It seemed like that was the epitome of the ranch, to blend into the surroundings. Sure, all the buildings she saw, and there were more than she originally noticed, were impressive, but they looked as if they belonged with the surrounding nature. Not forcing their presence on the land, but becoming one with it.

Samantha rolled her eyes. That was so cheesy, she just needed to stop. She rushed to catch up to Zeke, who was halfway around the fountain and heading toward the oversized four-car garage. When she caught up, he started firing words.

"The only one missing from the group right now is Jake. He's out on assignment up in Aspen." Zeke opened the side door into the garage and motioned her in. "Your apartment is up the stairs."

Samantha entered the garage and did a double take at the four cars parked there. She didn't know much about vehicles, but they all looked nice and new. She focused on moving her feet up the stairs, peering over the railing at the immaculate garage. Tools of all kinds lined the walls. Maybe one of the guys could get her car running again. Her heart eased at not seeing any calendars or posters of women in swimsuits. When she reached the top of the stairs, Zeke squeezed passed her and entered a code on the keypad on the door handle.

"The code is 9467. All the houses have codes to them that everyone knows. If there's an emergency, we all need to get somewhere without breaking down a door. But we can change yours if that makes you uncomfortable." He opened the door.

He stepped back and motioned her into the apartment. Her heart rate picked up as she moved past him. She couldn't stop the gasp that escaped her mouth. An enormous living area opened up to a wall of windows that overlooked the mountains in the distance. A sleek kitchen with an island and tall chairs was tucked neatly to the side. The room was fully furnished in dark brown leathers and rich fabric that left her with a sense of home she hadn't felt since her mom died.

"There are three bedrooms and two baths. Anything else you might need, just let me know. I'll go grab your stuff. Why don't you look around and see if this will work for you?" Zeke's footsteps tapped down the stairs, the fading sound creating a twinge in her heart.

"Get a grip, Sam." She huffed to herself.

There was no way she would let her heart get all dramatic over Zeke. He was her boss now. Plus, she had promised herself she would never fall in love with a man whose job put him in danger. Hearing her mom's sobs late in the night and finding her clutching Sam's father's picture as she slept had solidified Sam's determination. She couldn't have her heart end up shattered like her mom's, especially when she had Eva to think of. With that reminder, she pushed away any fluttering Zeke caused in her chest and explored her new home with delight.

CHAPTER SIX

Zeke leaned back in his office chair—Samantha's chair since she started working—as he stared at the numbers on the spreadsheet she had created. He couldn't believe everything that she had done in the last week. Not only was she able to get accounts to balance in a way that he could look at the piece of paper and understand what it said, but she'd also organized the office and their clients, and had baked a different cookie every day since she got here. She still claimed she had a few weeks of going through his massive amounts of receipts to get truly set up, but she impressed him none the less.

He took a deep breath and instantly groaned. Her citrusy scent filled his head and relaxed his muscles. While he was glad that he had hired her, the constant assault on his senses had him hunkering down and turning grumpy. He tossed the papers onto the table and stood to pace.

The night she moved in, he had brought the team up to speed about her situation. He'd tasked Rafe with garnering information about the Payne family and seeing what he could track down on their involvement with Samantha. He told the rest of them to keep their eyes out for anyone who might come. Goosebumps still rose on his skin when he thought of someone going to get Eva from daycare. He was glad Samantha had agreed to let Eva stay there while they figured out exactly what was going on. They had also contacted a lawyer friend of his who could help Samantha through this mess.

The report from Rafe hadn't been good. It appeared the Paynes were buddies with some shady people Zeke and the guys had the pleasure of dealing with while in the Unit. While the Paynes were old money, their wealth tracing back several generations, Kevin Payne's last decade had deviated far from his family's tradition of oil. From all the records, it appeared they were used to getting what they wanted. But Zeke wouldn't let that happen with Eva.

As long as Samantha worked with them, he could keep them protected. If she ever left and moved on to somewhere new, he would help her create a fresh life that would keep her hidden from the Payne's reach. He took a deep breath, pushing aside how that thought constricted his lungs and made it hard to breathe.

Laughter pulled him from the office to the living room. When he saw no one, he followed the sound out the screen door and onto the balcony. He couldn't remember the last time a sound so pure had surrounded him. That was a lie. He knew exactly the last time he'd experienced such joy. He'd spent long hours and many years trying to escape those specific memories.

The sound of giddy squeals punctuated his trek to the railing. He smiled at the sight of Eva running around the yard with Samantha, Sosimo, Rafe, and Derrick. Somehow the squirt had talked them into playing freeze tag, and they looked ridiculous, frozen in different positions across the yard. He laughed as he walked down the stairs to the sitting area around the fire pit. He sat in the chair and leaned his arms on his knees.

"Zeke, help!" Eva yelled through her giggles, as she ran away from Rafe.

"I'm just here to watch. You go ahead and play." Zeke sat back in the chair and crossed his ankle on his knee.

"Come on, Zeke. Come play tag with us." Rafe smiled at Zeke and waved him over.

Zeke shook his head and crossed his arms.

"Stop being such a pansy. It's just a game of tag." Sosimo smirked as he egged Zeke on.

"Says the man standing on one foot with his leg sticking out like a ballerina," Zeke countered.

Rafe growled loudly and lunged after Eva, pretending to miss and fall on the ground. She squealed in delight and ran toward Zeke. She got to him and grabbed his hand. Her pleading, big blue eyes crumbled all his resolve.

"Please, Zeke, I can't get them unfrozen without your help." Eva pulled on his hand like her tiny form could make him stand.

Zeke dramatically huffed, then sprang up with a roar, hauling Eva up into his arms and taking off away from Rafe. Eva's delighted screams pierced his ear, but he didn't care. The way her body jumped as she giggled loosened something around his heart he hadn't realized was tight. They ran to Sosimo and unfroze him before racing in the other direction.

Next he ran toward Derrick, frozen with both hands on the ground and his hind end up in the air. Zeke burst out laughing as he whacked Derrick's butt, sending him sprawling into the grass, and took off across the yard toward Samantha.

"Go, Zeke, go," Eva yelled in his ears. "Get Mommy."

"You're going down," Rafe said as he closed the distance between them.

Zeke glanced back to see how close Rafe was. When he turned back around, Samantha's eyes widened, and Zeke realized he'd miscalculated the distance to her. He tried to stop but slid right into Samantha. He wrapped his arms around her and, as they fell, twisted so that both she and Eva landed on top of him.

Eva scrambled out of his arms and took off running. "You'll never catch me, Rafe."

"I still have to find your wings, fairy princess," Rafe said as he ran past Zeke and Samantha, throwing Zeke a wink.

Samantha pushed up and peered into his eyes. She tilted her head, and her eyebrows drew together.

"Are you okay?" Her breathless voice and slight weight kicked his heart rate up higher than the mad dash had.

Zeke nodded as he tightened his hands around her waist. The closeness of her sweet citrus scent exploded all rational thought from his head. She scrambled off of him and reached her hand down to help him. He grabbed on to it and let her help pull him up. They stood there staring at each other. Zeke shook his head to loosen his thoughts. Her eyes grew wide, and she ripped her hand out of his before running away.

"Run, Zeke," Samantha yelled over her shoulder.

Run was right. Zeke didn't want to have long stares into her eyes or his heartbeat quickening with the touch of her hand. He couldn't let himself fall for another woman with a kid. Last time he had, it had nearly broken him to pieces. He'd have to remember to keep the walls firm around his heart, not letting Samantha and her daughter breach his defenses.

SAMANTHA SAT on the couch in the main house, her feet tucked up under her and a hot cup of tea in her hands. Zeke sat on the floor in front of her with Eva on his lap, playing poker with the guys around the coffee table. Sam needed to start taking Eva to their apartment earlier in the evening and let the guys have time without having to entertain a four-year-old.

Each night she told herself that during dinner. But each night she held off. She loved the sense of family these four men had—and that's what it was, a family. It made her realize just how alone she had been over the last four years. She shook her head. She knew that wasn't true. She'd been lonely most of her life.

Growing up, she'd often wondered why her mother preferred to spend time with the kids at Children's Mercy and not with her own daughter. Sam had spent many evenings wondering what those children had that fascinated her mother, trying to figure out if she could capture some of their magic to get her mom to come home before nine at night. Even on her mom's day off, the phone had often interrupted whatever they did, dragging her attention away from Sam. She'd never admit that in her loneliest times she'd prayed to get sick so she could get some of her mom's focus. It never worked. She had a rock-solid immune system.

When she got old enough, she volunteered at the hospital, figuring if her mom couldn't come home, then she'd go to her mom. It was then that she understood the draw of the children who needed her mom's expertise so badly. It had still hurt, and the solitude had stung, but Sam had at least realized it had never been about her or what she lacked. Then, after her mom had died, Sam truly was left with no one. So while she knew the guys probably wanted time sans kid, she couldn't bring herself to pull away.

Zeke leaned back against the couch, and his shoulder touched her shin. The touch sent shivers racing up her leg and into her core. She hugged her mug of tea in her hands and tried to ignore the way the simple touch, one he probably wasn't even aware of, lit her up like the Fourth of July. So what if his touch sent her popping? The last thing she wanted was a relationship now. Besides, he probably didn't even like her, if his distant manner said anything.

That wasn't true. He liked her enough as an employee, but as a friend? She doubted it, which meant her racing heart every time his cologne hit her nose had to stop.

She blamed her hypersensitive hormones on the stress of the last few months and the fact that she finally didn't have her stomach rubbing against her backbone. She loved her new job, the challenge of it, but if she didn't get her little crush under wraps, she'd have to find another place to work. Because there was no way she'd hang around when he didn't feel the same. Look where that had gotten her with Garrett.

Loud groaning from around the table drew Sam's focus. Eva snatched all the pretzels from the middle of the table while the others threw their cards down. She turned around in Zeke's lap and gave him an enormous hug.

"We won." She bounced up and down and turned to the other guys, pointing her finger at each of them. "Read 'em and cry like big babies."

Everyone burst out laughing. Sosimo turned his head and spewed soda all over the hardwood floor, which made everyone laugh even harder. Sam's heart just about burst from the joyful moment. She got up and grabbed paper towels from the kitchen. As the laughter died down, Sosimo took the towels from her hand, a huge smile on his face. She snatched her mug and went to get more tea. She loved it here with this family. She would not ruin it by making things uncomfortable with Zeke.

As she made her way back to the couch, the front door opened. A man carrying a large duffle walked in, a slight limp to his gait. A large scar ran from his hairline, down his cheek, and through his beard. He looked exhausted as he dropped his bag in the entry and surveyed the room.

"Jake," Derrick hollered, waving him in from where he was dealing another round. "Thought you weren't coming home until tomorrow?"

So this was Jake, the last man of the team. He'd been out on an extended job, so Sam hadn't met him yet. On par with the rest of the guys in the house, he was built, tall, and far too good-looking. Did they only accept hot guys in the Special Forces or what? His face held a hardness the others didn't, not even Zeke.

He shrugged and headed toward the kitchen. "They didn't need me, and I was ready to sleep in my bed." He opened the cupboard and pulled out a glass.

"Jake, this is Samantha and her daughter, Evangeline. Samantha's our new office manager. They're staying in the apartment," Zeke said as he organized the cards in Eva's hands and whispered into her ear.

Sam turned from the touching scene and smiled at Jake. "It's nice to finally meet you. Can I warm you up something to eat? Derrick made amazing steaks for dinner."

"Nah, I'm fine, but thanks." Jake filled his cup at the sink and took a deep drink. "So, Zeke finally caved and hired someone?"

Sam shrugged as she slid onto a stool at the kitchen island. "Yeah, well, him hiring me was more out of pity, but I hope I've been able to help him out."

"How's that?"

"Zeke was at my last job when I got fired. Add to the

mix my ex's family has gone psycho, and Eva and I kind of got pushed on Zeke."

Sam inwardly scolded herself. Why had she even said such a thing? Sure, her living in the apartment above the garage was an act of mercy, but she'd helped Zeke out just as much. His disastrous books were now balanced, and his office, that had looked like a bomb had exploded, she'd efficiently organized. Jake hadn't asked for any information, and yet here she was, giving him her whole sob story. The warm fuzzies of this family and her depressing mental trek down memory lane had her mouth spouting things she never would before. She needed to just head home while she was ahead.

"Huh." Jake cocked his eyebrow and set his cup on the table. "Well, glad you're here and can get Zeke out from behind the desk."

She nodded and forced a smile. She took her mug to the sink, rinsed it out, and put it in the dishwasher. Jake limped over to the living room and placed his hands on his hips.

"You want dealt in?" Derrick asked as he shuffled the deck for another round.

Jake shook his head. "I think I'm just going to go turn in."

"Debrief in the morning." Zeke didn't even look up from his cards when he issued the command.

"Yep, sounds good."

"All right." Zeke glanced up and nodded at Jake. "Glad you're home, man."

"Yeah, me too. I'll see you all in the morning," Jake

said over his shoulder. He turned toward Sam, where she still stood in the kitchen. "Glad to meet you, Samantha."

"Sleep tight." Sam cringed as Jake chuckled.

Sleep tight? He wasn't two. She needed to head to her place.

She finished wiping the sink and dragged herself into the living room, reluctance to leave sitting heavy on her heart. Rafe elbowed Sos and pointed his cards toward Eva. Sam followed their gazes and froze. Eva had fallen asleep in Zeke's arms, half a pretzel hanging from her lips and her arms wrapped around his arm in a hug. Zeke glanced up at Sam, their gazes holding. A soft smile lifted his lips, and the tension normally on his face disappeared. Her chest swelled so much she didn't think she could take a breath.

She cleared her throat and gathered Eva's backpack to get her bearings. "I should take her and get her to bed."

"Here, I'll take her over for you." Zeke stood and adjusted Eva in his arms.

"I can get her."

"Sam, I've already got her. Maybe she won't wake. Go get the door."

He had never called her Sam before. She nodded woodenly, trying not to read too much into it.

"Good night, guys." She waved at them and turned to leave, trying to tamp down the ember his words had sparked.

"Sleep tight." Rafe's singsong voice made her flush.

She glanced over her shoulder and stuck out her tongue. Now she acted childishly like Rafe. Oh, brother. Rafe waved his fingers at her and winked. She laughed and turned back toward the door. The laugh dried up in her throat at Zeke's pursed lips and the way his gaze darted between her and Rafe from where he stood, waiting.

"Sorry." She rushed over and opened the door.

"No worries." His voice rumbled as he passed by her, closer than necessary. Or was that just her imagination?

Samantha turned one last time to wave to everyone before following Zeke out the door. It surprised her to find him waiting for her on the landing. She pulled the door closed and headed down the stairs.

Only the crunching of their feet on the rocks disturbed the silence of the night as they walked across the drive. The air seemed heavy between them. She wrapped her arms around her as the chilly fall air pierced through her sweater.

"Was Jake hurt? He was limping." She couldn't help but fill the hushed tension.

"No, he was injured a year and a half ago during a rescue mission we did with the Unit. Lost the bottom half of his leg. Most of the time you wouldn't notice, but when he's tired or sore, he limps slightly." His voice held a hint of concern.

"Oh," she said feebly.

She picked up the pace and opened the door to the garage so that Zeke could go in. Then she ran up the stairs, punched in the code, and held the door open again, feeling like one of those guys that greeted visitors of those fancy hotels. She chuckled to herself and shook her head as she closed the door.

"What's so funny?" Zeke stood near, looking at her, his brow furrowed slightly.

"Oh, nothing, I was just thinking about how I felt like a cartoon character running to open doors for you." Samantha shrugged and pulled her sleeves down over hands to cover her nervousness.

Zeke hadn't been up to their apartment since the first day he helped carry her stuff in. His presence made the large space seem small.

"Where do you want this little nugget?" He tilted his head to Eva.

Sam startled, her body heating at just standing there looking at him. "She's right back here."

Duh, he didn't know what bedroom Sam had put Eva in. Out of the three bedrooms, she'd placed Eva at the end of the hall. It had seemed safer that way.

She led him down the hall and opened the last door, crossing the threshold and turning back Eva's covers. Zeke sauntered in, stepping carefully around the toys the guys kept buying Eva scattered on the floor, and gently laid Eva in her bed. He pushed her dark curls out of her face before stepping back.

Samantha swallowed the lump in her throat and pulled the covers up, gently kissing Eva's forehead before following Zeke out of the room. She closed the door, taking care to not let the door slam. When she turned to go down the hall, she bumped into Zeke, her palms splaying his solid chest to steady herself. His hands caught her upper arms, and he took in a deep breath.

Before she could put too much thought into his

touch, she stepped back and wrapped her arms around herself. "Sorry, I didn't realize you were there."

"Could we talk for a minute?" He cleared his throat before motioning down the hall.

"Sure, no problem." She fiddled with the cuff of her sweater as she walked down the hall and into the living room, wondering if she'd done something to upset him. She stopped in front of the living room windows and gazed out at the moon as it reflected off the pond. Maybe if she focused on the scenery outside, her nerves wouldn't jumble all up in her throat.

"I wanted you to know that you're wrong." His low, rich voice kicked her jitters into overdrive as he stepped close.

She glanced up at him. "What do you mean?"

"When you told Jake I only hired you out of pity. That's not the truth. I needed your help just as much as you needed mine." He stared out the window, his cheek muscle jumping as he clenched his jaw.

"Okay."

He turned his gaze down at her and stared into her eyes. She swore he must've moved closer because the back of his hand brushed hers, shooting infuriating fire up her arm.

"Are you adjusting okay out here? We aren't over-whelming you too much?" Zeke asked quietly.

A smile bloomed on her face, and she sighed. "I love it here. This family you've created. It's overwhelming at times, but it's unlike anything I've ever had before. So, yeah. I'm adjusting okay." She shrugged and turned her gaze back outside. "I keep telling myself that I should leave after dinner, bring Eva here so you guys can have some quiet without her bugging you all the time. But each evening when dinner finishes, I can't seem to pull myself away. I guess I've just been lonely for too long, and I'm sucking up all this friendship like a desert in the rain. Wow, that was really sappy." She turned a laughing smile up at Zeke.

His eyes widened as he rubbed his hand on his neck. The air caught in her chest. Had she said too much?

He touched her shoulder and gave a soft smile. "I'm glad you feel that way. If you didn't hang out after dinner, one or more of us would probably show up, asking if Eva could play. She's just too much fun to have around."

He dropped his hand quickly and took a small step back. She was both relieved and frustrated by the distancing action. She told herself that this was what she wanted, for things to not get complicated.

"You're great with kids. You've got her eating out of your palm. Did you have a lot of siblings growing up?" Samantha grabbed a basket and started filling it with the few toys that had migrated to the living room, hoping the action would cool her body.

"No, my ex-fiancée had a daughter. Must've gotten enough practice with her." The way he cleared his throat and turned away made Samantha wonder if he meant to tell her that bit of information.

"Well, Eva sure loves you. It's good for her to be around all you guys."

Zeke started picking up toys with her, and their hands brushed as they each dropped one in the basket at the same time. They both froze. Only this time, he didn't step away. He stared down at her, his mouth opening as if he wanted to say something. His eyes quickly darted to her mouth and back up, and he took a step away. Clearing his throat, he began walking backward toward the exit.

He opened the door and paused. "Thanks for all the work you've done this week, Samantha. You're a good addition to the team."

She nodded, and he left the apartment with a soft click of the door. She thunked the basket of toys on the coffee table and slumped into the armchair, throwing her arms across her eyes as she sank back. What in the world just happened? He hadn't looked as unaffected and distant as he had the rest of the week. Could it be that she might not be the only one feeling all hot and bothered? She stood and went to her bedroom, thinking a long shower would clear her mind of whatever that just was.

CHAPTER SEVEN

Zeke stomped down the hall toward the office, realizing his terse attitude was firmly back in place. He had his phone in his hand as he read the email from the building contractor again. How could he have done such a bone-headed thing like not paying the man?

"Saman—"

"Shh." She grabbed his arm and startled him.

Why was she standing next to the door like she was hiding? Her hand left his arm tingling as she pointed to the open window, then held her finger to her mouth. He could hear Jake's clipped tone coming from the porch, but not the words.

Samantha leaned toward him, rising to her toes. "She insisted that he read her the book about the frog and the princess." The soft breath of her words on his neck caused moisture to fill his mouth.

He swallowed. "Really?" He had worried what Eva's reaction to Jake would be, with his scarred face and back-off demeanor.

"I was going to go save him, but next thing I know, she's up in his lap and he's reading her the story." She brought her fingers to her lips, hiding her smile, and leaned back against the wall.

He leaned against the doorjamb, listening to the low cadence of the story. The stress of the last few minutes melted away as the heat of her presence warmed his side. He relaxed into the feeling. Eva sighed dramatically, and he smirked.

"I just adore princess stories." Eva's high-pitched voice came through the open window clearer than Jake's.

Samantha's shoulders jumped up and down, and she shook her head. Zeke glanced at her, and she mouthed "adore" before hiding her mouth behind her hands again. Laughter looked beautiful on her.

"Adore, huh?" Jake's voice held a lightness Zeke hadn't heard since the mission that had changed all their lives.

"Yep." Eva sighed dramatically. "Jake, are you a prince?"

Jake's choking laugh caused Zeke to squeeze his lips tight to keep from bursting. "No, Eva, I'm not a prince. Why would you ask that?"

"Because you're pretty like a prince," Eva said dreamily.

"I'm not pretty … not anymore." Jake's voice was thick with emotion.

"Oh, yes, you are. You're the prettiest in all the land."

Zeke met Samantha's gaze. Her hazel eyes glistened brightly, and a quivering smile tipped her full lips.

"Jake?"

"What?"

"When I get older, I'm going to marry you." Eva's declaration and Jake's sputtering response had Zeke doubled over in silent laughter.

Samantha giggled softly and leaned closer, her words barely a whisper. "I think you've been replaced."

"Story of my life," he whispered back, his lips brushing her curly hair that smelled like vanilla and oranges.

Now why did he say that? He straightened and shook his head.

"Cap, we have a problem." Derrick's words as he marched down the hall dried up all of Zeke's laughter. "There's a Kiki here to see Samantha."

Samantha's eyes went wide as they swung from Zeke to the window. She swallowed and turned to Derrick, who stepped into the office.

"Where is she?" Sam's voice was firm and full of strength.

"In the living room." Derrick tipped his head down the hall.

She nodded and pushed passed him, marching with determination. Derrick clapped him on the back, then followed Samantha. Zeke wasn't sure what this Kiki was playing at, but he wasn't going in unprepared.

"Jake, take Eva to your place and don't be seen. Keep sharp," Zeke called out the window to Jake on the porch, then rushed down the hall when he heard Jake ask Eva if she wanted to meet his pet dragon named Rex.

Zeke slowed as he came around the corner. Derrick leaned against the couch, appearing casual, though Zeke knew Derrick could jump into action in a split second. Samantha stood with her arms crossed, tapping her foot. Her stiff shoulders radiated nervousness, but she looked burning mad. Kiki was petite, maybe only a bit over five feet, with brown hair cut in a sleek bob. The same startling blue eyes as Eva's peering from the woman's face left no room for imagining this wasn't her aunt. While Eva had Samantha's defined cheekbones, darker skin, and beautiful, curly black hair, it appeared the girl got the Payne eyes and stubborn chin. The light from the opened front door sparkled off Kiki's flashy jewelry.

"What are you doing here, Kiki?" Samantha's glacial tone was one Zeke had never heard before.

Kiki held her hands up in surrender. "I just wanted to make sure you were okay and see Evangeline, if you're not opposed."

"Oh, I'm opposed, all right." Samantha uncrossed her arms and pointed at Kiki. "You honestly think I will let any of you see her after the crap your family pulled?"

"I can't imagine how you feel." Kiki lowered her hands to her side.

"You can't imagine how I feel? Really? Well, let me tell you." Samantha took a step closer, her hands clenched at her sides. Zeke moved up behind her, mostly to show his support, but also just in case she hauled off and attacked the woman. "First, that lovely brother of yours laughed in my face when I told him I was pregnant, said it served me right for being so stupid and not being on the pill."

Samantha's hard laugh slammed into his gut like a rubber bullet. If Garrett was alive, Zeke would track him down and beat the snot out of him. From Derrick's stiff expression, he wouldn't be alone.

"He was right, of course, I should've known better. That was the last I heard from him. He didn't even respond to my email when I reached out to him after she was born." Sarcasm thickly laced her words. "Stupid me, thinking a dad might want to meet his daughter."

"That's how we found out. Your email was still in his inbox when I went through it after he died." Kiki held her hands in front of her, slightly wringing them together. "My parents are excited about Evangeline. We all are."

"So excited you'd do anything to take her away from me?" Samantha's hand trembled with emotion by her side. "When I wouldn't bow down and grovel at the Payne's throne, you took everything from me."

"What?" Kiki touched the base of her neck and swallowed.

"People started whispering every time I went somewhere. My boss said having me work there was like having the plague, even though I'd been a stellar employee for the last three years." Samantha's voice was rising. "And when all that didn't work out to your advantage, my landlord evicted us. Can you imagine my surprise when I went to get money out of my account to put a deposit down on a new place and my accounts were all frozen?"

"I ... I didn't know." Kiki appeared genuinely surprised, by her soft whisper and shocked expression splashed across her face.

"Just my luck, I picked one of the banks your father sits on the board of, huh?" Samantha took another step closer. "Then again, it serves me right for being so stupid."

Kiki's face paled, and her eyes darted around the room. Something wasn't right. Zeke's body warmed, and he glanced at Derrick, whose eyebrows squished together.

"So tell me again, Kiki, why are you here? Why would you even think about showing your face after you tried to kidnap my daughter from daycare?"

"What? No!" Kiki sputtered.

"Go ahead, Kiki, tell her what we are doing here." A man dressed in an expensive suit strutted in, a gleam in his eye as he surveyed the room. Zeke knew this type of man—all polish, but no real shine.

Kiki flinched, her eyes widening a split second before a mask of indifference covered all her emotions. The motion had all of Zeke's warning bells ringing. He took another step closer to Samantha and placed his palm on her lower back for a second to reassure her.

"Gregory, what are you doing here?" Kiki cocked her eyebrow, her tone icy. "I told you I would handle this."

"Protection, cousin." Gregory motioned to Zeke and Derrick. "We don't know what kind of men Samantha has now embedded herself with."

Samantha sucked in a breath. All of Zeke's muscles tensed at the slimeball's words. He stepped up beside Samantha and crossed his arms.

"You have two minutes to state why you're here before I remove you from my property." Zeke unclenched his jaw and forced the words out as calmly as he could.

"Listen, it's simple." Gregory sneered before sighing

dramatically. "Garrett's parents just want a chance to talk to Samantha, to show their regret in this misunderstanding. They're waiting to have a video chat."

Samantha clenched her hands and growled. "Mis— misunderstanding? Why you—"

"Derrick, get Rafe on the line. Have him set up the TV so we can have ourselves a little chat." Zeke narrowed his eyes at Gregory. "Tell him to double time it."

Samantha turned to him, her mouth falling open. He gently grabbed her arm and pulled her into the kitchen. She shook under his hand, so he loosened his grip and rubbed his thumb up and down her soft skin on the inside of her elbow. The hair on his arms and neck rose as his callused skin bumped over hers. She took a deep, shuddering breath and crossed her arms, pulling from his grasp.

He cleared his throat and pitched his voice low so the Paynes wouldn't hear. "Listen, if we talk with them, we can figure out what their angle is. Right now, we're flying blind. At least, after we talk, we'll know their game."

"We'll never know their game. Not really." Her voice shook as she stared at Gregory and Kiki, who talked in low tones by the front door. Sam pulled her lower lip between her teeth and bit on it.

"Sam, please, trust me on this." Zeke kept his hands bunched at his side, though he wanted to rub her shoulders in comfort and give her a hug. Gregory's words still burned hot in his ears, and Zeke didn't want to give any evidence the jerk's innuendo was correct.

She tore her gaze from the unwanted visitors and stared up at him. "I trust you." The firm confidence in her voice exploded warmth into his chest that shot down his arms.

His muscles tightened as he leaned in. "They will not get Eva. I promise you that."

She closed her eyes and took a deep breath through her nose. His brain ran a rapid replay on all her words to Kiki. Sam didn't deserve this, didn't deserve their strong-arming. He was glad she and Eva were here, that he and the guys could help her after all she'd gone through alone. The Paynes may be powerful and used to getting what they wanted, but no one messed with his family.

His heart took off with that thought as he looked down at Sam. Somehow during the last three weeks, the Jones women had woven into his family as thoroughly as any of the others. He wasn't sure what he thought about that beyond the need to protect them, but knew no matter what, he and the other guys would do whatever they could to keep them out of the Paynes hands.

CHAPTER EIGHT

Samantha marched to a chair in the living room and eased into it. She attempted to act as frigid as possible, though her insides skipped and twisted like an acrobat. Zeke came up and stood next to her, his arms crossing his chest. Her arm still tingled where he had held it earlier. The roughness of his thumb had sent her stomach into a riot for an entirely different reason. She had pulled away, needing to be strong.

"We're all set here." Rafe looked up and nodded at Zeke.

She appreciated that Derrick had stayed and was sitting in the other living room chair. She smirked at the fact that Kiki and Jerkface had to sit on the couch. The minute Gregory had sat down, he'd fallen back into the deep cushions, his eyes flying wide. He then scooted up and sat on the edge of the couch, his elbows leaning on his knees. Sam would've laughed at his ridiculous expression under any other circumstance, but now she just wondered if they'd ever get his stink off the cushions. She was glad she chosen the chair. It gave her a slight sense of control.

"All right, Rafe. Put in the call." Zeke's calm voice eased some of her tension.

She knew she could do this, especially with the support of Zeke and the guys. She never would have had the courage to do this on her own, but she also wouldn't have had the power to either. She figured if anyone could go up against the Paynes, Zeke Greene could. She had found out just these past weeks how much power he truly had. Not only did he have enough money to rival the Paynes with his accounts totaling in the billions, but he had the moral compass to go up against them on principle. She knew without a doubt that he would help her and Eva, even if she wasn't working for him or wasn't friends with Chase and Beatrice. If she had come to him as a stranger, he would've helped. That was just the kind of guy he was.

She gazed up at him, her heart in her throat. He glanced down. His gaze connected with hers, and he gave her a quick wink before turning his attention to the screen where Kevin and Cynthia Payne popped up.

Samantha stifled the urge to shift in her seat. The presence of money leached through the screen with their outfits that probably cost more than everything Samantha had. She swallowed the bile that rose up her throat. Kevin smirked while Cynthia tapped her perfectly manicured fingernails on the top of the oversized desk they sat behind.

"Why don't we go ahead and get this started?" Kevin leaned forward in his chair and rested his arms on his obnoxiously ornate surface. "Mr. Greene, it appears my granddaughter is being held captive in your facility. We'd like to bring her home where she belongs."

Samantha sucked in a breath at the audacity of the man to not even address her personally.

"Mr. Payne, I have no say in Miss Jones's whereabouts. You'll have to talk to her mother about that." Zeke's voice held steel as he dropped his arms and stuck his hands in his pockets.

Kevin rolled his eyes and turned to Samantha. "Are we done yet? Are you ready to stop this ridiculousness? All we're asking for is a chance to be part of Evangeline's life. Is that too much to ask?"

"You never gave me the chance to decide for myself. When I showed any hesitance, your attacks started almost immediately. Why would you think I would let my daughter around the likes of you?" Samantha prayed that her voice would stay steady.

"Darling, you misunderstood us." Cynthia placed her hand on the desk and looked sympathetically through the screen.

"You Paynes seem to like that word. I'm not sure how you'd think I could misunderstand when everything you did was bent on destroying me."

Kevin tsked. "Do you honestly think you can provide for Evangeline? We could give her the world. All you can give her is a tacky secondhand unicorn backpack and rice and beans."

Samantha's heart raced at his words. They'd been watching her for longer than she thought. "It doesn't matter if I can provide fancy clothes or everything she wants. She has a roof over her head, clothes on her back, and food in her belly. I'm her mom, and you have no say in what happens to her."

"Father, is it true you froze Samantha's accounts and had her fired?" Kiki twisted her ring on her finger. Sam wasn't sure what to make of her. She had seemed genuinely surprised when Sam had told her everything her family had done.

"There was suspicious activity on her accounts." Kevin shrugged.

"Sweetheart, it was for her own good." Cynthia's sugary tone made Sam nauseous.

Kiki burst from the couch. "For her own good! How can you say that attacking a single mom is for her own good?"

"That's about enough out of you, young lady." A vein popped from Kevin's forehead. "If you do not hold your tongue, Gregory will escort you to the car."

Kiki threw her arms up and paced behind the couch.

"I'd like to know the answer to her question." Zeke's low voice had Sam peeking at him from the corner of her eye. He was a mass of controlled anger—an incredibly handsome mass with his dark piercing eyes and a short beard that did nothing to mask his clenched jaw.

"I'm sorry, Mr. Greene, what was that?" Kevin's confused act fell short.

"I'd like to know how you can justify attacking an innocent woman? Did I talk clear enough for you?" Zeke asked in a tone that had goosebumps covering her arms and relief rushing through her body that she wasn't on the receiving end of his anger.

"It wasn't an attack, but an opportunity for her to realize all we can do for her." Kevin straightened in his chair.

"To me, not for me. You and your family have done nothing for me." Sam dug her fingers into the chair's arms so she wouldn't burst from her seat as well. "This conversation is over. I will never let my daughter be tainted by you."

Sam sat back in her chair and folded her hands in her lap. Cynthia gasped, and Kevin's face turned a brilliant shade of red. Gregory glared at her across the coffee table.

"Tainted? That's laughable coming from you. You realize that your parents were nothing but orphans, raised in foster care because no one wanted them, right?" Kevin sneered and barked a laugh. "Your father's own drunk of a dad killed himself after killing your grandma for cheating and your mother's mom was nothing but a druggie who died from an overdose. And you're saying we would taint Evangeline? She's already saturated in your under-privileged filth. We're trying to do her a favor."

All feeling rushed from her, and she was thankful that she sat. How did he know all of that about her family?

"Let me make one thing crystal clear." Zeke stepped forward. "Miss Jones is an amazing mother. Your *son* waived his rights to *his* daughter when he refused to acknowledge her existence. You will give Miss Jones access to all her accounts you froze and refrain from contacting her or her daughter again, and we will forget this ever happened. But understand that if you continue to harass Miss Jones, I will make your life a living nightmare."

Kevin chuckled unpleasantly. "I don't think you and your little rent-a-cop team can handle me."

Rafe stood and moved beside Zeke. "I believe the Vice President and Secretary of Defense would be very interested in your funding of weapon manufacturing in the Middle East."

Kiki gasped, drawing Sam's attention to her. Her blue eyes were bright against her reddened eyelids, and her pallor was pale. Sam stood and moved next to Zeke.

"Or what about his ongoing conversations with strategic Russian diplomats?" Derrick asked, crossing his ankle over his knee like he didn't have a care in the world.

"I don't know what you are talking about," Kevin scoffed and leaned back in his chair, his Adam's apple bobbing.

"We may just be rent-a-cops, but I can guarantee you, if you continue to come after Miss Jones and her daughter, I will make it my mission in life to take you down," Zeke threatened with such menace that Sam didn't doubt he'd die attempting to fulfill that pledge. "We're done here."

Rafe clicked a button, and the screen went blank. Silence weighed heavy in the room, except for Kiki's shallow breaths. Zeke exhaled and lowered his arms to his side. The back of his hand touched Sam's, and she leaned into it.

Kiki ran her hands through her hair, pulling it before dropping them to her sides. "Samantha, I'm sor—"

"We're leaving." Gregory interrupted Kiki, grabbing

her roughly by the elbow and yanking her toward the front door. He snatched her purse from the table and turned back to the room. "You have no idea who you are dealing with."

Kiki's face held a mixture of disgust and pain as he pulled her out of the house. Sam followed them and stood on the top stair. Kiki yanked her elbow from Gregory's grip and snatched her purse from him before marching to her own car. Sam wasn't sure what Gregory was saying to Kiki as he followed her, but from Kiki's expression, it probably wasn't good.

Sam clenched and unclenched her hands as they hung by her side. This entire experience had her burning hot and sick to her stomach at the same time. That she saw Garrett's same cockiness in Kevin and Gregory's demeanors made her wonder what she had ever seen in him. She probably was stupid.

Zeke stepped next to her, his hand rubbing up against hers again. "You okay?"

Sam nodded and cleared her throat. "Thank you."

"We're here for you, Sam, no matter what happens." Zeke's low voice soothed all her nerves.

Tears stung sharply in her eyes, and she blinked rapidly to keep them from falling. Zeke's finger tapped hers. Sam closed her eyes, held her breath, and slid her hand into his palm. For a moment, Zeke didn't move, then slowly he threaded their fingers together and held on. The connection lightened her, as if the mountain sitting on her shoulders had lifted a little. She exhaled deeply and opened her eyes. Maybe now, everything would be all right for once.

THE NEXT DAY, Zeke marched into the office and stopped short. Samantha sat in the desk chair, chewing on the end of a pencil as she scrunched her nose at the computer. She'd pulled her hair up in a messy updo with black curls and half a dozen pencils poking out from it.

She looked beautiful with the sun shining on her dark skin. He wondered if it would be warm if he rubbed his fingers where the sun hit. His fingers tingled with the thought. He took a deep breath to focus and immediately had her joyful scent invade him. The sweet smell evoked images of sunshine and fresh beginnings and was perfect for her.

He shook his head to loosen his brains. He came in here for a purpose and it wasn't to contemplate how she smelled like joy. The facts hadn't changed—she was still a single mom, and he had no interest in going there again.

Liar.

"Samantha, let's go." Zeke cringed at his gruff tone. Just because he was upset at himself for acting like a randy teenage boy, didn't mean he had to act like a jerk to her.

She startled, dropping her pencil from her mouth as it hung open. She saw him and relaxed. She chuckled softly and smiled. "I didn't see you there."

So much for her having the same reaction to him as he had to her. She walked into the room, even if it was behind him, and—boom—senses on high alert. Shoot, she just entered the house, and he somehow knew she was there, like some twisted sixth sense meant to drive him wild.

He took a few steps into the room and crossed his arms. "Can you turn that off, please? I need you to come with me."

Her perfectly shaped eyebrows pulled low over dark hazel eyes. "I'm trying to figure out the different classes for the purchases so we can organize them better." She gestured toward the computer and cocked an eyebrow. "Remember, you hired me to get your accounts all cleared up."

"Yes, and you are doing a wonderful job at that." He moved around the desk and leaned his hip against it. He was far too close to her but couldn't seem to force himself to move away.

She sat back in the chair and crossed her arms. "And where are you dragging me off to?"

He leaned forward and pulled a pencil from her hair. She froze, her eyes wide, her breath catching.

"The stables. I want to work on your self-defense and practice shooting." He pulled another pencil free.

"I don't need that. I already know how to defend myself." Her low voice trembled slightly. "Besides, I'm here. With you."

She pulled her bottom lip between her teeth, drawing Zeke's attention to how kissable they were. He swallowed and leaned a little closer, twirling a curl through his fingers as he slid another pencil out.

"You won't always be here."

The air stilled between them as her breath hitched.

She rolled the chair back and stood, glancing out the window.

"You're right." She yanked the rest of the pencils out of her hair, tossed them next to the computer, and skirted the desk on the opposite side of him.

She stomped out of the room without a look back. He shook his head, trying to remember what exactly he had said to get her all riled up. All that came to mind was how he loved the feel of her curls twirling around his fingers and how if she hadn't stood, he probably would've leaned in and kissed her. Not exactly a brilliant way to keep his distance.

Ten minutes later, with his racing heart somewhat back to normal speed, he stood in front of Samantha. Who was he kidding? Lately, his heart was never calm around her.

"Okay, we're going to work on how to get away if someone grabs your arm." Zeke's eyes narrowed as she rolled her eyes.

"Zeke, this isn't neces—"

"It's completely necessary. I want you able to fight if someone comes at you." Zeke used his command voice. She crossed her arms and glared. "Now if someone grabs your arm, take a hold of their hand with your free one, point your elbow up, then slice down toward your core. It'll break the connection so you can run." He did the motions himself while he talked. "Let's try."

He grabbed her wrist loosely. She did exactly as he had said, breaking his hold the first time. After making her do it a few more times to make sure she had it, Zeke was confident to move on to harder moves.

"Good." He smiled and nodded. She huffed. "Now, if someone grabs you by the throat." He stepped up and softly grabbed her neck.

He felt her swallow. His fingers tingled where they touched her skin. Her breath shuddered as she exhaled. He rubbed his thumbs along her jaw.

"Don't worry, Samantha. I won't hurt you."

"We'll see," she whispered. He flinched and opened his mouth, but she cut him off. "Are you going to hold me here all day or what?"

Zeke snapped his mouth shut and focused. "Okay, if someone has you like this ..." The thought of that chilled Zeke to the core. "Then you lift your arm up, turn your entire body to the opposite side to break the strength of the hold, and strike your elbow to their face." Zeke dropped his hands. "Why don't you choke me so I can show you?"

"I think I got it." Samantha smirked. "Choke me."

Zeke lightly put his hands around her neck. A second later, she had her elbow to his face. His eyes widened in shock.

"Yeah, I think I got it." Samantha stepped back and wiped her hands together.

Zeke cocked his eyebrow. "Right. Let's try something different. I'm going to come at you. I want you to defend yourself. Okay?" Samantha nodded. "Just act like you're walking down the street."

Zeke backed away until there was a good fifteen feet between them. Her lips tipped up on one side before she schooled her expression. He ambled toward her, then dashed the rest of the way, reaching out his arm to grab her. To his surprise, she stepped into his approach, pushed his arm out of the way, and stars exploded in his brain.

———————

"ZEKE, WAKE UP."

Why was Samantha in his room? Her hand rubbed against his cheek and down his neck, lighting his body on fire and thrumming through his brain. While the initial touch woke his body, it also woke his brain, which was pounding in his head. Why was he on a hard floor?

"Zeke, please wake up." Samantha brushed her hand over his cheek again.

He opened his eyes and gazed up at the stable ceiling. Oh yeah, he'd been teaching Samantha. Had she really knocked him out? He groaned and sat up, his head spinning wildly.

She kneeled right next to him, her eyes bright with tears. "I'm so sorry. Are you okay?"

Placing her hands on either side of his face, she turned his face this way and that. He grabbed her hands and pulled them to his chest. He shook his head, that still spun like he'd just ridden the teacups at Disney, and leaned closer to her.

"I tried to tell you." She sighed and clenched his hands.

"Tell me what?" With her this close and his head still clearing, he was having a hard time focusing.

"I don't need training in self-defense." She quirked a

tiny smile before sobering. "I have a black belt in Kajukenbo."

He let out an airy snort. "You don't say."

She shrugged. "My parents grew up in a rough neighborhood. My mom wanted to make sure I could defend myself if something happened."

"Well, you certainly can do that."

"I've never had to use it before. Sometimes I worry I wouldn't. Then I go and knock you out cold." She shivered. "I hate violence."

He moved so both her hands were in one of his and used his free hand to push some loose curls behind her ear. He trailed his hand down the side of her neck until he cupped her head. Man, she really was amazing.

"I'm sorry I didn't let you talk." He rubbed his thumb over her cheek. It was as silky as it looked. "Why don't we swing by the sick bay so I can grab some pain killers then move on to the shooting range, unless you're already a marksman as well."

She shook her head. "I'm not too fond of guns, either. Not with how my dad died."

"What happened to him?"

"He was killed by enemy fire during a deployment overseas."

Zeke's heart clenched, and he dug his hand into her hair. "He was in the military?"

Samantha nodded, meeting his gaze. "Army Ranger."

Just. Great. Zeke blew out a breath, closed his eyes, and leaned his forehead on hers.

"I'm sorry." He couldn't think of anything else to say.

"I barely knew him. He died when I was Eva's age."

Her sigh blew against his neck and caused his hair to rise. "My mom never recovered, crying herself to sleep most nights even fourteen years later. Told me to never fall in love with a man whose job puts him in danger."

She pulled away slightly. Her hazel eyes bore into his as her fingers flexed in his grip. Zeke's every nerve ending fired in rapid succession.

"I'm starting to doubt if she was right," she whispered before kissing him softly on the cheek. "Come on. Why don't you teach me to shoot?"

Before his thoughts could catch up, she pulled away. When she stood, she reached her hand down to help him up. Even though it went against every thought screaming in his head to pull her back close and kiss her, he let her keep her distance. But there was one thing they seemed to have in common—he was doubting his logic in staying away as well.

CHAPTER NINE

Zeke leaned against the kitchen counter, drinking his cup of coffee and watching Eva pick out all the marshmallows from her cereal to eat. His cheeks hurt from trying to keep his smile contained. He rolled his head and shoulders. His muscles screamed from when Samantha rang his bell the day before.

Teaching her to shoot had been a lesson in restraint, which he hadn't failed. But he hadn't aced either. His body heated just remembering the feel of her cradled between his arms as he helped her hold the gun so she could shoot. He may have stood closer than necessary. Inhaled her sweet scent like he was a starving man standing outside a barbecue joint with no funds to go inside.

"Ugh, really?" Samantha stomped in from the office. "Who gave her this junk?"

Zeke's eyebrows winged up, and he shook his head and shrugged. "Wasn't me."

"Ah, come on, Mom. That cereal is part of a balanced

meal." Sosimo brought his own bowl from where he sat in the living room going over their next job with Jake and Derrick, and sat on the stool next to Eva. "It says so in the commercials."

"Sos, we're going to the doctor's office for a check-up! Now she'll smell like a sugar factory." Samantha grabbed a paper towel, got it wet, then marched around the island. She gave Sosimo, who was drinking from his bowl, a whack as she passed, causing him to spill sugary pink milk down his front.

Zeke chocked out a laugh, barely keeping his coffee from shooting out his nose. Samantha peeked over at him and gave him a half-smile and a wink before turning back to cleaning Eva up. His stomach flipped and twisted like it did before a mission. She really did fit in here.

He stepped up to the sink on shaky knees and rinsed his coffee cup. "I'll be taking you today. We can leave whenever you're ready."

She smiled, and his chest heaved. "You don't have to."

"I know." He held her gaze until her smile stretched wider and she ducked her head.

Rafe came rushing into the room with his computer. "Guys, you have to see this."

He turned on the TV, and his desktop and all his icons showed on the big screen. Zeke moved around the island to stand next to Samantha. Eva stood on the stool and lifted her arms to him.

Scooping her into his arms, he nuzzled her neck with his beard. "Mmmm, you smell sweet. I think I might have to gobble you up." He made munching noises as he tickled her.

"No, Zeke." Her laughter spread warmth in his chest.

"Knock it off. This is important," Rafe hollered, the serious side he rarely showed surfacing. "I was going over the security feeds and found something you need to see."

The room quieted as everyone leaned forward. The screen filled with Zeke grabbing for Samantha. Her movements were so quick, he barely saw her palm swing up and connect with his face. In the feed, he fell to the ground like a cut tree, bouncing as he hit the floor. Rafe beamed at him as the guys erupted in shocked expressions.

"How'd you do that?" Derrick gaped.

"Did you see him fall? Classic." Rafe laughed.

Samantha turned a pained expression his way. "Sorry," she whispered.

"Man, Zeke. You got a headache today? Because she knocked you clear into next week!" Sosimo bent over laughing.

"Look! He's still out cold!" Jake pointed to the screen, his face split into a rare smile.

They all turned to the TV. Sure enough, Zeke lay on the ground with Samantha bent over him. The counter on the video feed read two minutes.

"Wait. I slowed it down." Rafe clicked on his computer.

Before Zeke could protest, the feed changed to him stepping up, his arm moving upward in super slo-mo. Her jaw steeled in determination. Zeke sucked in a breath at the strength her beautiful face exuded. She stepped into his body, pushing his reaching arm aside, and, in excruciating slowness, her arm rammed into his chin, snapping his head back. His body crumpled and flopped like a marionette whose strings had been cut.

"Ooooh," echoed through the room as everyone turned eyes full of admiration to Samantha. She fidgeted, her dark cheeks turning a deep red.

"Did you all catch Zeke's face?" Rafe cued it back and pointed at the screen. "Right ... there."

The shock on his face was comical the split second before he dropped. Zeke stifled a chuckle.

"Mama, why'd you hit Zeke?" Eva hugged his neck tighter. "Miss Patti says hitting isn't nice."

His heart exploded with her protectiveness.

"I know, honey. I shouldn't have hit him like I did." Samantha put her hand on Eva's back, brushing his hand in the process. She gazed up at him. "I really am sorry."

He shrugged. "I deserved it." He patted Eva's back. "I told your mom to do it, squirt. She was teaching me a lesson on how to listen and not be such a bossy man."

Eva snuggled into him. "I don't think I like that school very much."

Zeke laughed and hugged her tight, his heart freezing then jumpstarting at the rightness her defense brought to his spirit.

Jake approached them, his expression serious. "Where'd you learn that?"

Samantha shrugged. "Kajukenbo. It's a Hawa—"

"Hawaiian form of martial arts that mixes a bunch of practices," Jake finished for her with a smile. "I've done some."

"She's a black belt." Zeke's chest expanded with pride in her.

Samantha smoothed her shirt, then shoved her hands in her jacket pockets.

"Do you think we could spar? I'd love to learn some techniques taught in that discipline." Jake pushed his hand through his hair.

Sam's eyes went wide before her mouth spread into a pleased smile. "Yeah, sure. I'd love to do that."

"Hey, I want to learn how to take Zeke out with one hit, too!" Rafe yelled from where he played the punch on repeat.

"She can teach all of us her spidey secrets later. We have to get to the doctor, and you all have a job to get to." Zeke placed his hand on Sam's lower back and guided her toward the attached garage. The touch sent tingles up his arm.

He smiled in satisfaction as the guys all groaned and picked up their stuff. She snatched up her purse and Eva's backpack as they passed a side table and glanced up at him with a smile.

"Why are they muttering like cranky three-year-olds?" Samantha stepped into the garage and walked around the front of the Bronco.

"This job is some fancy three-day charity event up in Aspen. There's usually a lot of prep work, but not much action. Added to that, they're not happy since they'll have to stay there the next two nights."

The rest of the morning went by uneventfully. Zeke waited in the doctor's lobby while Samantha took Eva back for her appointment. He'd only had one kid come and ask him if he was a professional wrestler or something. He chuckled as the mother rushed up and apologized as she pulled the kid away. Now Zeke, Samantha, and Eva sat in the Glenwood Canyon Brewpub waiting for their lunch to arrive. Eva had begged to sit next to the window so she could watch if any trains came through. So there they sat, squeezed into the crowded area around the bar, at a table up against the window.

He couldn't help but stare as Samantha helped Eva with a maze on the kids' menu the waitress had given them. Sam glanced up at him and smiled softly before turning back to the paper. The simplicity of the moment displaced something in his heart, like shifting blocks until they fell into place.

He wasn't sure when his thoughts had veered, but they now settled firmly into the possibility of a life with these two. Not just at work as part of his team. He fidgeted, his lungs having difficulty breathing. Could he open his heart up again? Was he really considering placing himself in danger like that? Samantha and Eva laughed and shared a hug when they finished the maze. The noise of the busy brewpub fell away to the happiness of this thought. Yeah, the risk would probably be worth it.

The waitress came with their meal, and Eva clapped in delight at the smiley fries lined up next to her cheese pizza. The rich aroma from his French dip instantly made his mouth water.

Eva squealed and pointed out the window. "The train. Look, Mommy, the train." The train pulled up to the depot across the street, and Eva pressed her hands and face up against the window so she could watch.

"You guys picked the perfect time to have lunch," the

waitress said as she placed Sam's salad on the table. "The train leaves every day at 12:10."

"I want to ride on the train someday." Eva's eyes were still wide with awe.

"Someday, baby," Samantha said as she pushed her salad around on her plate.

"I told you to get a sandwich." Zeke took a big bite out of his and groaned dramatically. He spoke around the bite. "So good."

She reached over and snagged his other half.

"Hey!" Zeke protested.

She took a bite and closed her eyes, nodding as she chewed. "I should've listened to you."

"We could share. Split our meals in half." Zeke motioned to their plates.

"You'd do that?"

"For you? Yeah." Could she see that he meant much more than sharing a meal? That he would do just about anything for her?

She held his gaze, her expression softening. "Thanks."

He tore his gaze away and pushed his plate against hers to transfer some of his fries. Shuffling his foot, he accidentally knocked up against hers. Instead of pulling away, he kept his foot there, leaning it into her. She looked up, a question on her face.

He slowly smiled, his heart racing in his chest. "Sorry." He wasn't sorry at all.

"It's okay." Her breathy and low voice eased into his chest.

Eva turned around, her body fairly brimming with

excitement, and dug into her lunch. She started chattering around the food in her mouth. Samantha shifted, and just when he thought she would pull her foot away, she leaned it more solidly up against his. His lips tweaked into a smile as he chomped onto a fry. This was turning out to be a fantastic day.

SAMANTHA SQUINTED at the cards in her hands, trying to remember all the rules to this game. She wasn't succeeding very well. Not with the memories of the day bombarding her mind. She thought about how Zeke had split meals with her, putting the au jus dip in between their plates so they both could dip. Then, when they'd walked across the bridge to show Eva the Colorado River, she hadn't missed the sense of family that had overwhelmed her and caused her eyes to tear up. Thankfully, she had blamed it on the cold, autumn air that blew strong on the bridge.

Zeke had played with Eva all afternoon while Sam had gotten some work done. Their laughter and chatter had wrapped around her heart and lodged there. She hated to say that she had gotten little work completed, what with all her inner debating going on.

She glanced at him across the coffee table. He had a slight smile pulling up one side of his mouth. He was gorgeous, with his dark brown eyes that lit up every time he saw her daughter. Eyes that seemed to penetrate her soul as he stared at her. She pulled her sweater away from her body twice to cool off.

Zeke shift his cards in his hand, his forearms flexing as he did. She had never really cared much about big muscles, but on Zeke, they equated warmth. Safety. She desperately wanted to know what it felt like to have his powerful arms wrap around her. Not just while he was instructing her to shoot, though how she'd hit anything with his scent twined so completely around her, she'd never know. No, she wanted to experience what it felt like to be captured in his arms for the sole purpose of holding her. She wanted to trace the ridges of his muscles and the design of his tattoos with her fingertips. Whew, it was getting hot. She fanned herself with her cards.

"Are you hot? I can turn the fire down." Zeke moved to get up, and she grabbed the leg he had stretched out under the table.

"No, I like the fire. It's homey." She shrugged and reached for the hem of her sweater. "I think I just need to lose some layers. My Texas blood can't decide what to do with this Colorado weather."

She pulled off her sweater, glad she had worn a tank top underneath. When she got herself situated, she glanced across the table, her mouth frozen open to tell him something witty. His stare took her all in, from the top of her head to the tip of her fingers and back up again. It wasn't the lusty looks she got from men, even Garrett when they'd been together. No, Zeke's look was warm and left her feeling cherished. She loved that feeling. Her heart hammered in her chest.

"Mama, it's almost my song." Eva stood and wrapped her arms around Sam's neck, breaking the connection that tethered her to Zeke's stare. Sure enough, *The Princess and the Frog* movie was to Eva's favorite part.

"Your song?" Zeke asked as he set his cards on the table.

Eva scurried over Sam, kneeing her in the face and pushing her head back to get to him. He laughed, then covered it by looking stern.

"You just about trampled your mom, squirt." He easily caught Eva as she tossed herself into his arms.

Sam wondered if he'd catch her if she did the same.

"Sorry, Mama." Eva barely acknowledged Sam before turning back to Zeke. "Mama said she thought the name in the song was beautiful, and that I was sure to light up the sky and shine bright like the moon."

"She was right. You shine so bright it almost hurts to look at you." While his smile was big, Sam wondered at the emotion in his tone.

"Dance with me." Eva jumped up and pulled on his arm.

"Dance with you?" Zeke made a face. "I'm not so good at dancing."

"That's okay. I'll teach you."

Zeke stood up fast, scooping Eva into his arms. She shrieked and hugged him tight. As he twirled with her—Eva's smile large and happy—pain radiated from Sam's chest and brought tears to her eyes. She blinked rapidly, grabbing her cup and going to the kitchen. She needed distance, space to catch her breath from the scene before her. She knew what it was like growing up without a father. Though Sam tried to be with Eva as much as she could, making sure her daughter never felt the loneliness that had defined Sam's childhood, she also knew there would always be a hole not having a father created. A safety she remembered from her vague memories of him.

She filled her cup with water, gulped half of it down, then pasted on a smile as Eva called her over.

"Mama, come dance with us," Eva cried out as Zeke spun her around and lifted her high in the air.

"Oh, no." Sam moved back to the living room and placed her cup on the side table. "Three's a crowd and all that."

She bent to sit when a strong arm snaked around her waist. The smoky, earthy scent of Zeke and Eva's bubble gum ice cream surrounded her in a delicious combination. Her muscles relaxed into the pull of peace that surrounded her, and she stiffened her muscles with a jerk, placing her hand on his chest to steady herself.

Eva sighed and placed her head on Zeke's shoulder. "So this is what it's like."

Zeke shot Sam a questioning look. She shook her head and shrugged.

"What's like?" he asked, jiggling her with his arm.

Eva giggled and wrapped her arm around Sam, including her even more into the embrace. "What that family in my movie feels like."

Zeke's eyes widened, and his muscles tensed. Sam's stomach hardened in dread. What would he say? She moved her mouth to say something, but her words froze in her throat. He gazed at Sam, his body loosening slightly as he nodded. His hand inched up her back.

His eye contact didn't waver as he swayed to the

movie's music. "Yeah, squirt. This is what family feels like."

"I love it." Eva nuzzled into Zeke's neck.

Sam watched in fascination as Zeke's Adam's apple bobbed up and down. His chest expanded as he inhaled, and, as he exhaled slowly, he closed his eyes and pulled Sam up against him. She squeezed her eyes shut against the sting of tears and laid her head against his neck. His heart pounded against her hand in a frantic pace that matched her own. They continued to sway long after the firefly's song ended.

CHAPTER TEN

Zeke laid a sleeping Eva into the tent he'd set up for her in the third floor sitting area. When he had first suggested they stay in the main house for the weekend since the guys were all gone on the job in Aspen, he had only been worried about their safety. He felt much better with her under the same roof, even though they were on the top floor and his living quarters were in the basement.

For some reason, one he wasn't willing to explore too deeply, he didn't worry as much when Sam and Eva were snug in their place with the guys at their own. But with all the guys away for the job, Sam and Eva had seemed too exposed without the team protecting their flank during the night. Now he wondered if he'd ever be able to relax when they went back to their apartment.

He ran his finger along Eva's sweet cheek, pulling his hand back and making a fist. He crawled out of the tent, making sure to not make any noise. Then he stood there staring, wondering what it would be like to tuck her into bed each night. What it would be like to actually be a family rather than to just feel like one.

Sam stepped up next to him, her presence expanding his chest even more. "Zeke? Is everything okay?"

He scrambled for something to say that wouldn't expose his train of thought. "Will she be all right here?"

"Are you kidding me? You saw how thrilled she was with this setup." Sam's quiet voice filled with laughter.

"But what if she wakes up in the middle of the night? Won't she be scared?"

"With how busy the day was, she'll sleep clear through to morning. Besides, I'll leave my door open. If she wakes, I'll hear her." She grabbed his hand and pulled him toward the entryway.

When she loosened her hand to break the connection, he squeezed his. She glanced down to their joined hands, and his heart raced like he'd just ran three miles through the jungle ... while being chased. She raised her gaze to his and cocked an eyebrow.

"Are you tired?" He rubbed the back of her hand with his thumb, sending sparks shooting up his arm.

Her "no" came out more breath than voice as she shook her head.

"Will you sit with me for a while?" He held his breath.

She nodded, and lightness filled him until he felt weightless. He led her downstairs and pulled her to the couch. He motioned for her to sit and had a sense of loss when she pulled her hand out of his. He gathered his courage and situated himself in the middle of the couch instead of the opposite end, laughing at himself when it took almost as much nerve as when he would breach buildings full of enemy combatants.

Sam bit her bottom lip, distracting him so much that he almost missed her question. "What happened with your ex?"

He jerked and leaned away, his mouth going dry. His thoughts rushed for a way to not answer the question without being rude.

"I'm sorry. I shouldn't have asked." She twisted her hands in her lap. "It's just that you know everything there is about me, and I know nothing about you."

Guilt slammed into his chest. If he wanted to explore the possibility of something more with her, he had to open up. He swallowed the rock in his throat.

"She decided she wanted a different kind of family than I could provide her."

Sam's forehead furrowed.

He sighed and ran his hand over his head. "She met this guy who was better situated than I was, so while I was deployed, she left and got married. Sent me an email telling me we were done."

"No." Sam covered her mouth with her hand.

"I never saw her or her daughter again."

"But you're loaded." She whacked both hands over her mouth, and her eyes widened.

Zeke laughed and grabbed her hands away from her face. He traced the lines on her palm. "I wasn't always loaded. That actually just happened two years ago. It's been a blessing in setting this business up the way I want to, but I'm glad I didn't always have it. I might've ended up like Gregory Payne."

"You'd never be like that." Her insistence warmed him more than the citrus sunshine of her scent.

He squeezed her hand and leaned closer. "Why not?" His voice came out gravelly.

She shrugged. "Maybe you would be, but it's hard to imagine. You're nothing like Garrett or Gregory." She groaned. "I just need to zip my lips."

He grinned, thinking he knew the perfect way to do that.

"I just wish Chase had ended up being Eva's father, then this whole mess would've gone away." Sam leaned her head back against the couch.

Her words cooled the fire burning through his veins, and he lowered his eyes. "Why did you wait so long to have Chase get tested?"

"It was hope, the massive hope that my calculations had been wrong." Her laugh was self-deprecating. "I always was too good at math." She cleared her throat and turned to him. "So I know your grandpa left you a boatload of money. Were you close with him? What about your parents? Where are they?"

"My dad and grandpa didn't get along, so I wasn't able to see my grandpa much. It's kind of sad since my dad's an only child and so am I. You'd think they could've put aside their differences."

"You'd think so, but I'm not the best judge of what family would do."

"You're a great mom to Eva." He squeezed her hand.

She lifted her face to him. "Thanks." She smiled, and the world fell out from under him. "What about your mom?"

The question slammed him back to reality. He cleared his throat. "She left when I was nine. Decided she wanted a new family. I guess that's the story of my life."

"What? Why would she do that?"

"To be fair, she and my dad never really got along very well. She got pregnant while they were dating, and they got married. Then she met someone she fell madly in love with, so she left. She was tired of all the arguing."

"Where is she now?"

"California, I think. After she left, I went back and forth between the two houses. But my stepfather already had kids, and I didn't fit in with her new family." Zeke went back to tracing the lines in her palm. "After a couple of years I stopped going, and she stopped pretending to care. My dad and I have a solid relationship, though. I could always depend on him, and my stepmom Jodi is amazing, sending me care packages with essential oils and homemade cookies."

"Is that why you smell so good?" She sniffed deeply, closing her eyes.

Zeke's mouth went dry. "Yeah. She worries about me. Sent me some roller bottle full of vetiver and sandalwood. Said it would ground me, calm my nerves. It actually helped, so she's been supplying me ever since. She sends unique blends to the guys, too. Makes them call her Mama J."

"I love it, love the way it wraps me in warmth when you're near." Sam sighed and leaned into him, placing her head on his shoulder. "I'm glad you had them. I didn't really have anyone, not really. My mom was so busy at the hospital saving lives that she never had time for me. When she died in the car crash, I really found out how stifling loneliness could be. I never want that for Eva."

He turned his face, his lips brushing against her hair. "She's lucky to have you."

She shook her head and stared into his eyes. "No, I'm blessed to have her. She's everything to me. I would do anything to keep her safe and loved. Anything."

His breath caught at her ferocity, at her warrior spirit that fought her enemies and conquered them. He leaned forward and brushed his lips against hers, sending a jolt through his body.

"I don't want you to have to do that alone anymore," he whispered against her lips.

She took a shuddering breath in before leaning forward and kissing him softly. His heart beat wildly in his chest, thumping loud in his ears. He pushed his hand into her curls.

He deepened the kiss and swore he'd experienced nothing so confusing and incredible at once. His mind raced with possibilities, but her presence filled him with peace. It left him burning yet shivering. He didn't want her to be alone. He wanted her to be with him.

"Are you seeing if Zeke's a prince?" Eva's giddy voice ripped them apart.

Sam's eyes flew wide as she glanced from her daughter to him and back. "What are you doing up?" Her voice squeaked and made him want to pull her near again.

"I'm thirsty." Eva pointed at Zeke. "So is he a prince?"

Sam's lips turned up in a telling smile. "Yes, he's a prince, all right."

"Wahoo. Now you can get married." Eva threw up her hands in celebration.

Sam sputtered and scrambled off the couch. "Dear Lord, help me not sew her lips shut," she mumbled as she rushed around the couch. "Your water bottle is upstairs. Now, say good night to Zeke, young lady, and I'll take you to bed."

"Good night, Zeke," Eva said in a singsong voice. "I can't wait for you to be my daddy."

Sam gasped and pushed Eva toward the stairs. She turned around and mouthed, *sorry*, before whispering low to Eva.

"Good night, squirt."

He couldn't tell her yet that the thought of being her dad filled him with so much joy he thought he'd burst. He still wasn't sure what to think about that, but he planned on taking the few days the guys were away to evaluate contingencies and formulate a plan.

SAMANTHA PAUSED in her inputting and listened to the low muttering and giggles coming from the front area of the house. Her neck and cheeks still warmed when she thought of being interrupted by Eva the night before. She'd played the scene again and again in her head until she finally had fallen asleep somewhere around two. Now her mind was sluggish and still bent on repeating the night before on a continuous loop.

She smiled, touching her lips with her fingertips. She didn't mind admitting that she spent most of her time rehashing the kiss that exploded her brain into a million pieces. She was honestly surprised that she'd been able to react as quickly as she had when Eva interrupted them, because a few seconds earlier, her intelligence had been reduced to nothing more than heat and fireworks. It all started with him tracing her hand in delicious slow circles that sent sparklers up her arm.

She huffed and shook the receipt before her, as if the motion would focus her dreamy thoughts. Zeke had told her she didn't need to work today, but the mountain-high stack of papers she still needed to go through had her itchy. Since she had taken most of the previous day off for Eva's appointment, she didn't mind putting in a few hours. She read the list of supplies bought and gasped when recognition dawned. This was a receipt for ammunition. Her eyes widened as she scanned the sheet. Lots and lots of ammunition.

She willed her muscles to relax as she typed the information into QuickBooks with short, jerky motions. They ran a security firm. That meant they would need to have a way to keep their clients safe. It wasn't like they were going out looking for danger. Though if someone was hiring security, there was most likely a reason for concern.

When Zeke had explained what they did, it sounded like mainly setting up elaborate home security systems and standing guard at social events. She should've realized it meant more.

She reached for the next receipt and relaxed when it

was customizations for the SUV. She inputted the information and placed the receipt with a satisfied slap into the to-be-filed pile. It was ridiculous how much pleasure she got from this kind of work, but she'd always loved the steadiness that numbers brought. She shook her head with a chuckle. What kind of person thought of math with such fondness? She shrugged, knowing there was no changing the logic of it.

With a smile, she grabbed the next receipt and froze. The paper shook so violently in her hand she thought it'd rip. She dropped it onto the desk like it was a snake and stared. The receipt was full of bulletproof attire from a specialty store. At least twenty different Level IV ballistic vests, whatever that meant. There were helmets, backpacks, casual vests, tank tops, parkas, hoodies, even Armani suits ... all bullet proof. The list had women's clothing as well. Ice raced through her veins.

She put her elbows on the desk and pushed her fingers along her nose and eyebrows. The action didn't relieve her tension like she hoped.

"That's exactly how accounting makes me feel, too." Zeke's voice held laughter, causing her to flinch.

She pulled her hands away from her face and sat back. She tried for a smile but must've failed by the way Zeke's expression changed from jovial to concerned in an instant. She crossed her arms to hide her trembling hands.

"What's wrong? You're chalky." Zeke strode around the desk and leaned against it so he was facing her.

Great. That's just what she wanted to hear. Not only

had he caught her having a moment of panic, but she looked atrocious having said moment.

She pointed with her chin toward the desk. "What's with the hundreds of thousands of dollars worth of bullet-proof tank tops? Where do you even store all that stuff?"

Zeke frowned and twisted to look at the paper. He shrugged and turned back to her. "We needed to prepare for any situation we might be in. We converted half of the stables into gear storage."

She thought of the long row of doors in the stables/shooting range and blanched. "Is what you do that dangerous?" She hated that her voice shook and clenched her jaw.

"No, most of the time not." He spoke slowly, like he was picking his words carefully. He reached out and grabbed her hand from her lap. "But I take our safety and the safety of our clients seriously. I do everything I can to make sure I protect us."

"What about the stock of bullets to supply a small army?" Why couldn't she just let it go?

"Too many missions in the military where our ammunition ran low, I guess." He pulled her up and eased her near, wrapping his arm around her. His closeness eased her nerves and slowed her racing heart. "Most of the jobs we do are easy. In fact, we haven't had a job yet where we've needed any of this. I'm just a good Boy Scout who likes to be prepared."

"I doubt the scouts were talking about Gucci Floral Bulletproof jersey jackets." She peeked at the invoice list as she pressed her palms to his chest. "I didn't even realize they made such things."

"The rich and famous like to keep their fancy styles, even when they need protection."

He turned serious, a furrow forming between his eyebrows. He brought a hand up her back and smoothed his thumb over her cheek. His hand cupped her neck, and he leaned forward. Could he feel her pulse picking up speed like a freight train?

"I promise you, safety is our primary objective, always." His low words raised all the hairs on her neck. "We have bulletproof clothing for ourselves in certain situations and for our clients who will need to blend in. That's not easy to do wearing tactical vests."

"Zeke, I thought you said you were getting Mama?" Eva's exasperated voice made Sam's neck grow hot with embarrassment.

Zeke's lips tweaked in a tempting smile before he winked and turned his head to Eva. "I am, squirt, but the princess needed some wooing."

Eva's pout bloomed into a smile. Samantha rolled her eyes. Great. Now he was encouraging her.

"Go make sure you have everything set out, and we'll be there in a minute." Zeke turned back to Sam as Eva ran down the hall whooping.

Sam lifted her eyebrow and flattened her lips. The vibrations of his chuckle singed her hands where they still pressed against his chest and sent another round of shivers cascading down her spine. He leaned forward, his breath raising those infernal hairs again.

"Come, my lady. Your lunch awaits." His whisper was low and husky.

He placed a soft kiss below her ear that liquefied her

knees before he pushed off of the desk and pulled her toward the doorway. It surprised her when her legs didn't collapse right under her, and she used her free hand to fan herself with her shirt. She'd have to change into something less stifling. She peeked up at Zeke. Or maybe keep her distance. He threw her a half-smile and winked. He glanced quickly at her lips before pulling her into the living room. Nope, not going to keep her distance. No matter how dangerous his job he might be.

"Mama, come look what we made." Eva ran up to them, grabbed Sam's free hand, and pulled her to the dining room table.

Zeke let go of her hand as she stepped up to a table set with candles. There were chicken nuggets and French fries on fancy china she hadn't seen yet and goblets of water with lemon sparkling in the sunshine. She whipped her head back to Zeke, her eyes wide with question. He toyed with his watch, fidgeting in a way she'd never seen him do before.

"It was Eva's idea." He cleared his throat and took a tiny step forward.

"This is amazing." She spoke past the boulder in her throat. "Thank you." She bent and gave Eva a hug. "Thank you, sweetie."

"I wanted it to be special, like when you used to set the table fancy at our old apartment." Eva squeezed her. "I loved it so much."

Sam never knew the cheap tablecloth and glass cups she'd gotten for fifty cents at the thrift store had meant so much. She had just been trying to find some beauty in the desperation that had settled over her, not knowing the "fancy" items would make such an impression on her daughter. She gave Eva another squeeze before she stood and turned to Zeke.

She stepped close, gathered her courage up, and gave him a soft kiss, placing her hand over his heart. "Thank you," she whispered against his lips.

He wrapped one arm around her and placed a longer kiss on her lips. "You're welcome." He bunched the back of her sweater in his hands before releasing her. "Squirt, where do you want us to sit?"

Eva jumped for joy and directed them where to sit. With a great flourish, she brought over a plate of cut-up fruit, only wobbling once. She beamed at them both, then climbed into her chair.

"Can I pray?" Eva asked. When both Sam and Zeke nodded, Eva folded her hands dramatically and squeezed her hands together. "Dear Lord, thank you for bringing us here. Please keep Jake and Rafe and Sosimo and Derrick safe."

Sam smiled at her concern for the others.

"And thank you for Zeke and Mama and that she found out he's a prince and can marry him now." Eva's words had Sam choking on her laughter. "In Jesus' name, amen," Eva finished with exaggeration.

Sam peeked across the table at Zeke, who had his lips pressed flat together. His eyes danced as he looked back at her. She pulled her lip between her teeth and bit it to keep from laughing. His gaze darted to her mouth, then back up to her eyes.

"That was perfect, squirt. Thanks." He held Sam's

gaze as he dipped a nugget in barbecue sauce and chomped it in half.

He should have looked ridiculous biting into a dinosaur nugget like that, but he looked anything but. Heart-pounding sexy? Incredibly so. She felt like the end of that *Inside Out* movie when the teenage boy's emotions were running around in chaos.

Sam lowered her eyes to her plate and willed her body to cool off. She was toast. Well and truly done in. Whatever had caused Zeke to turn all his alluring attention to her would be her downfall. She was pretty sure she'd enjoy the plunge.

CHAPTER ELEVEN

Zeke came down the stairs from the sitting area where he had been reading books to Eva. She had fallen asleep after the fifth one, so he had eased her down onto a pillow and tiptoed out of the room. He stopped short at the sight of Samantha standing at the door, her arms crossed. His heart beat double time.

"I thought you were told not to come back." Samantha's voice held an edge as hard as steel.

"I know. I know, but I was hoping we could talk." Kiki's voice came through the doorway.

"There's not much to talk about. Your family wants to take Eva away from me, and I'm not willing to let her go." Sam's foot tapped impatiently.

Zeke silently cheered at her gumption and stepped to the security screens in the hall to see if anything else showed up. Nothing suspicious appeared around the grounds, aside from Kiki standing at the door, her hands fidgeting in front of her. Gregory stood behind her, off to the side. He scanned the area like he expected someone to jump out of the bushes. Zeke smirked and slowly pushed his finger on the fingerprint keypad on the drawer below the screens. When it popped open, he pulled a handgun out, slid the clip silently into place, and tucked it into the back of his waistband, pulling his shirt over it. Closing the drawer, he made sure it locked and then ghosted across the room.

"No, it's not that ... It's just ...," Kiki's voice stuttered.

"Listen, Samantha." Gregory's placating tone scraped down Zeke's spine. "We'd take care of Eva and you. I'd take care of you." A pleading tone was thick in his voice.

When Samantha didn't reply right away, Zeke stalled in his approach. She lowered her head and closed her eyes. Zeke's blood froze in his veins.

She firmed her shoulders and lifted her head. "I don't need anybody to take care of me or Eva. We're doing fine, just like we've always done. I will never allow you guys to take her, so you might as well just stop trying."

Zeke stepped up behind her and grabbed the door. She jumped and turned wide eyes toward him.

"Is there a problem here? I'm a little confused, Payne." Zeke kept his voice calm, though his nerves zinged with unanswered doubts. "I thought we had come to an understanding. Miss Jones is not interested in anything the Payne family has to offer. I suggest you leave my property and the state."

Gregory took another step forward, his face turning red. "Are you threatening me?"

"No, I'm just telling you how it is. The snow hasn't fallen yet for skiing, so there's nothing left for you here in

Colorado. Unless you want to keep wasting your time and your money, you might as well head back to Texas."

Gregory turned furious eyes to Samantha. "Are you sure this is what you want to do?"

Kiki's face blanched as she looked at her cousin. She opened her mouth to say something, then squeezed it shut. Zeke still didn't have a read on her, but he sure as shooting had a firm understanding of Gregory.

"Oh, I'm positive I know what I'm doing." Samantha nodded as she took a step back into the house.

"Fine. I guess we'll be seeing you around." Gregory sneered before spinning on his heel and stomping down the stairs.

Kiki stared after him and shook her head, turning back to Zeke and Sam. "I don't know what he's thinking. And I'm sorry. I had hoped that maybe we could figure out some way that we could make this work. I'd like to get to know you and Eva." Kiki's voice trembled at the end before she cleared her throat, and with an apologetic look, she turned and followed Gregory to their car.

Samantha huffed, turned around, and stomped into the kitchen. Zeke watched at the door until the car drove away. He went back into the hall to check the monitors and make sure the Paynes made it all the way out the gate. He hoped they wouldn't have to lock the gate. He'd do it in an instant but wanted to avoid the hassle if they could. After the vehicle cleared the drive and sped down the road, he put his gun back in the drawer, closing it with a frustrated slap. He walked into the kitchen to find Samantha slamming cupboards and drawers.

"Ugh. Can you believe that man?" Samantha opened

another cupboard and then slammed it. "People like that just make me so mad." She opened another drawer, only to ram it shut.

Zeke chuckled. "What exactly are you looking for?"

She spun around, glancing at the kitchen and slumped. "I don't even know."

She sighed and covered her face with her hands. Zeke quickly approached and put his hands on her upper arms, rubbing up and down. Her shoulders shook with silent tears, causing a sudden coldness to hit his core.

"Hey, hey, it's okay. You don't have to worry about them. We'll take care of it."

"I'm not crying because I'm sad. I'm crying because I'm torqued off."

Zeke gently squeezed her arms. "Okay. I can understand that."

"Who does he think he is, coming in like that? He made me wanted to palm slap him like I did to you just to see him fly down the stairs."

Zeke burst out laughing as the tension rushed from him. The side of her mouth lifted in a half-smile. Her forehead furrowed, and she toyed with a button of his shirt. Heat sizzled from the contact, rushing through him, and driving out the cold her tears had caused.

"I've never wanted to hit someone before, not with such rage." She sighed. "I don't like feeling like that. I had to hold myself in because, knowing him, he'd probably sue and then where would I be? It's just so infuriating. I wish they'd leave us alone."

"They will, eventually." Zeke moved her tighter into his arms. "What if we take that bottled up aggression out on the shooting range? There's nothing as satisfying as filling a target full of holes."

She pressed her lips together in a slight grimace. The quiet "hmm" in her throat didn't elicit much hope she'd agree. If anything, it made him feel a little dirty, like the suggestion disgusted her. He stepped back, the heat in his body suddenly too hot and uncomfortable. He cleared his throat and grabbed his cup from the counter, downing the water in two gulps.

"I'm sorry. I've just never been at ease with guns." She crossed her arms and stepped back to lean against the counter. "Plus, I'm kind of worried I'll picture Gregory's face as I shoot." Her laugh sounded forced.

He set his cup on the counter with a thunk and really looked at her. Her ebony skin was flushed, and she fidgeted with the cuff of her sweater. He wanted to trust the hopeful feelings that stretched between them the last few days, but worried she'd leave him with his heart bleeding out from the hole she'd leave in his chest if she took Eva and moved on. He didn't know if he should thank Gregory or punch him in the face for pricking the bubble they'd been in.

"You realize that we use firearms in what we do? That to keep people safe, sometimes we have to use extreme measures?" He crossed his arms against the invisible cords binding his chest.

"I understand what you do." She met his gaze, taking a deep breath and letting it out. "I admire what you do. What you've built here. I know that your concern for others drives you to do the best you can to keep people safe."

She stepped across the open kitchen to stand in front of him. Her firm hold of his gaze the entire distance made his heart rate increase. He let his air out slowly through his nose to try to calm himself.

She stopped just inches in front of him and tilted her head back. "You're a man unlike any other man I've ever known. Taking in me and Eva even when you didn't want to. Making us feel as if we finally belong to something. It's what I admire most about you, your willingness to build a family even though your own was always strained."

A flush climbed up her cheeks as she took a step closer. Zeke tried not to hyperventilate. She pressed her hands against his chest, and his muscles twitched and zinged with the touch. She rose up onto her toes, her quick breaths just millimeters from his lips.

Sam bunched his shirt into her hands and pulled him the rest of the way to her lips. She kissed him with the deepness that matched his need and exploded any doubt in his mind. He grabbed her waist and pulled her close, pressing her against him as he angled his head to deepen the kiss. He inhaled her citrus smell, the joyful scent a reflection of his feelings. He didn't want to give in to his doubts and was determined to find a way to ease both their concerns.

SAM FLOATED across the driveway from the apartment into the house. Eva was happily playing with Tina, the nanny Zeke had hired to watch her during the day.

Sam had wanted to argue but realized that the guys couldn't always watch her daughter, and she didn't want to risk sending her back to daycare just yet. When he had shown her all the research he'd done on the young woman, how meticulous he had been in making sure she would be good for Eva, Sam had conceded. Her heart had filled with the warmth that could only come from being loved by someone as amazing as Zeke.

She skidded to a halt, her hand pressing to her stomach. She didn't know if Zeke loved her, but the possibility of it left her giddy. It certainly reflected her own feelings. She glanced around the yard, wondering when she'd allowed her heart to open to the possibility.

Shrugging, she continued her way to the main house. Mirth bubbled up inside as she realized her steps were much lighter than they had been a few seconds before. His concern wasn't necessarily for her. He'd put himself in harm's way if it meant it would save someone else.

Sam tripped over air as that realization slammed into her. The image of her mom curled on her bed crying invaded her mind. She closed her eyes. Had she really opened her heart to someone exactly like her father? Someone who would leave her more broken than when he'd found her?

She shook off the thought and rushed up the stairs, determined to keep her mind off such things. She pushed the door open to all the guys sitting around the coffee table in deep discussion. They had gotten back from their weekend job in Aspen and looked to be in the middle of a debriefing.

"She said this meeting shouldn't have any issues, but

she also doesn't want to take the chance." Sosimo walked a quarter back and forth over the back of his fingers, his eyebrows scrunched low over his eyes.

Zeke glanced toward the door as she walked through, his eyes lighting up when they connected with hers. He motioned for her to come and sit next to him on the couch and turned back to Sosimo. "What's your take on the situation?"

"I think Reagan wants to believe there's not an issue, but she's also not stupid." Sosimo rubbed a hand along the back of his neck, nodding to Sam as she sat down next to Zeke.

"Reagan, is it?" Jake whistled and winked at Sosimo.

"Oh, shut it." Sosimo tossed the coin at Jake.

"Who's Reagan?" Sam asked the room.

"Sosimo's girlfriend." Derrick's voice rumbled with contained laughter.

Sam pushed Sosimo in the shoulder. "You have a girlfriend?"

He rolled his eyes. "I don't have a girlfriend. Reagan is our client from this weekend. I pretended to be her boyfriend at the charity event she held. She wants us to come back up for a meeting she has with potential investors for an invention she's made."

"I had facial recognition pulling up background information from the feeds we had running." Rafe shook some Skittles out of the bag into his hand and popped them in his mouth. He pointed the bag at Zeke, the little candies clinging in his mouth as he spoke. "She might think there's not a problem, but not all her guests were cuddly teddy bears, if you get my drift."

"There is validity in her wanting beefed-up security for this meeting she's having." Jake motioned toward the papers strewn across the table. "Whatever it is she's created, it's drawing a lot of attention."

Sam pulled her legs up to her chest and wrapped her arms around them. She tried to look casual, like their conversation wasn't scaring the living daylights out of her, but she worried. Her hand shook as she pulled her sweater sleeves over her fingers. Zeke grabbed her hand and wrapped his arm over hers, pulling the cuff of her sleeve back and sliding his fingers through hers. The guys' eyes widened, but they quickly averted their gazes. All except for Rafe, who wiggled his eyebrows up and down at her.

"So we go into this meeting with the expectation of a confrontation." Zeke squeezed her hand. "We're taking every precaution necessary in this one. Full body armor under our suits, and I'd like to make Miss MacArthur wear one of our women's bulletproof items we have in storage."

Sosimo nodded and rubbed his hand across his jaw. "I don't know about that, boss. She might not be up for wearing a heavy suit jacket."

"That's why we have a wide selection of options for her," Zeke said.

"Wouldn't she be more concerned about her safety than what name brand she was wearing?" Samantha hated that her voice shook.

Rafe shrugged. "You'd think so, but some of these people with more money than they know what to do with get wrapped up in stupid things like that." Rafe motioned toward Zeke. "Take Zeke, for example. Ever since his gramps left all that money to him, he's refused to wear anything but Calvin Klein T-shirts and underwear. Just last month, we were out on assignment when he had a run-in with a bull that ripped his shirt clear off him."

Samantha's eyes went wide, and her body chilled with the thought of Zeke getting gored by a bull.

Rafe smiled big before schooling it with a *tsk*. "We ran down to Walmart to get him something, and it was like we were forcing him to wear sackcloth."

"As if." Zeke's voice grumbled low in his chest, vibrating against her arm.

"Geez Rafe, give the man a break. One gets used to the feel of silky soft cotton up against the skin, and it's hard to go back to regular old Hanes." The enormous smile that spread across Derrick's black face ruined his backing of Zeke.

Everyone laughed, and Sam marveled at how relaxed they were when the conversation was so serious. Her heart raced at the thought of them all in danger, and she wasn't sure how to slow it down. She forced a smile.

"All right, you've had your fun. We need to come up with a game plan." Zeke started circling his thumb along the back of Sam's hand as he spoke. The motion calmed her but also left tingles radiating up her arm.

"It won't be too hard to set up surveillance since we were just there." Rafe pointed to the blueprint on the table. "We can tap into the current existing network, beef it up some, and we'll have eyes on all the entrances."

"Miss MacArthur said she didn't want us to be standing there like bodyguards, but have us blend in to the meeting. She also wanted to make sure everyone would be safe." Zeke's voice held humor.

Sam inwardly scoffed. How could one expect to have security but not have it visible? It made little sense to her.

"That shouldn't be too hard." Sosimo shrugged. "Zeke, since you weren't there last weekend, you can pose as an attendee of this meeting. We can tell Reagan to have you sit next to her, that way you're close if something happens during the meeting. And with me pretending to be her boyfriend, I can sit on her other side."

Sam's heart flew into her throat at the thought of Zeke being there. She assumed he would stay behind like the last time. Her hands were slicked with sweat. Zeke leaned forward to look at one of the papers on the table, and she took that opportunity to pull free from his hand and cross her arms.

"That will work." Zeke looked around the table. "Rafe, you'll be our eyes and ears, monitoring the screens to make sure nothing catches us off guard. I'll be attending the meeting as an investor, and Jake and Derrick, we'll position you in the sitting areas outside the two doors. We keep this tight, and we keep focused. Got it?"

All of them nodded and began gathering the papers and gear. Sam stood and escaped into the office, not sure she could trust her voice to say anything. She couldn't do this, couldn't see them off like some homemaker in the Old West movies. While she meant to sit down and distract herself with work, she stared out the window at the serenity of the mountains outside. Aspen branches golden with fall foliage blew gently in the breeze. She focused on the movement and took deep breaths to ease the panic that rose up her throat.

Zeke's earthy scent filled her nose on her next inhale, causing her to tense right back up. His warm hand ran across her shoulder and cupped her neck.

"Are you okay?" The intensity of his concern had her shaking again.

"All of this just makes me nervous." Sam shrugged and turned to him. "I hate that I'm scared, but I'm not sure how to fix that."

"Don't worry about us. It may sound bad, but if we take all the precautions we talked about, there shouldn't be a problem." Zeke ran his hand down her back. "I want to show you how to work the gate. We'll close it behind us, so you'll need to know how to open it to let Tina out."

"Is that necessary?"

"I won't take any chances with you being here and all of us being gone."

Sam nodded and wrapped her arms around her. He pushed her hair out of her face and tucked it behind her ear before cupping the back of her head and pulling her in. She clutched his shirt, putting all of her anguish into her kiss, willing him to be safe.

When he leaned away, he smiled, gave her one more quick kiss, and led her out the door. "Let's go show you how the gate works."

She followed him down the hall, her emotions swirling in her head. His assurance had her wanting to believe him, but the memory of her mother's words echoed loud in her head.

CHAPTER TWELVE

Zeke pulled the SUV to a stop at the St. Regis Aspen Resort where the meeting with Reagan MacArthur would take place. She had explained that there were seven different potential investors lined up, and she'd be summarizing her invention. While the guys had said she'd detailed the charity event the weekend before down to the letter, her lack of information about her invention and this meeting had his skin crawling.

Of course, his nerves could be because of leaving Samantha and Eva back at the ranch. He squeezed the steering wheel to keep from checking the house security feeds to make sure that Samantha and Eva were okay. He'd spent the entire drive up to Aspen worried about if he had made the right decision in leaving them alone. He knew it was irrational. Samantha could easily take care of any problem that came up, but the thought of the Paynes doing something while he and the guys were gone had him wishing they had more security at his place. Or maybe a dog. A big vicious dog that loved little girls and protected gorgeous women from sleaze balls that wanted to steal them away. Okay, maybe he was being a little dramatic. He huffed as he opened the door with extra force.

"All right, let's get going. We only have two hours until the meeting to set everything up." Zeke motioned for the rest of them to get busy and marched inside to check in to his room.

He took the key to their room and had everyone load the gear from the back door so no one would observe them entering the hotel. As he slid his key card into the lock and pushed open the door, he remembered why he liked Aspen so much. The room was large with plenty of space. The hotel had set a sitting area up next to the large king-size bed. Though it wasn't on the upper floor, the view out the window was beautiful, overlooking the mountains that ran behind the hotel.

Maybe he would have to bring Samantha here. He bet she would enjoy the beautiful scenery and walking the streets of Aspen. He shook his head in disgust. They hadn't even talked much about anything permanent, so why was he suddenly jumping to taking her on trips? He was a goner.

As the rest of the guys went to the conference area to set up extra cameras, Zeke gave in to temptation and pulled up the app on his phone to check the security feeds at the house. He swayed slightly when the feed showed Samantha on the back deck, sitting with Kiki, enjoying a glass of lemonade. Eva played with Tina in the yard. He slumped onto the couch and took a deep breath to still his racing heart.

He would have to leave and figure out an alternative plan, because it was obviously a mistake for him to leave them alone. He quickly scanned through the other feeds, looking for Gregory. When Zeke didn't find Gregory, his eyebrows knit together. He switched back to the camera with Sam and Kiki, clicking on the sound and turning it up.

"... more than anything to be a part of Eva's life," Kiki was saying.

Samantha looked out at Eva over the porch's railing. "This has all been so complicated." Her voice had a hesitancy in it that froze Zeke to the core. "I wanted none of this to happen."

"I know. Me neither." Kiki sighed as she leaned forward in her chair. "Would it be so bad to let her family get to know her? That's all I'm asking."

Samantha didn't answer for a long time, and each second that passed nailed into Zeke's heart a little bit more. Was he going to lose her like he lost his fiancée, Gillian? Was he destined to make the same mistakes repeatedly? He ran his hand over his head, trying to stop the ache spreading from his chest.

"No, I guess you getting to know Eva wouldn't be a bad thing." Samantha's soft voice finally answered.

Zeke slammed his finger to close the app, wishing he hadn't listened at all. Guess that's what he got for eavesdropping. He squeezed his phone in both hands. What he wanted to do was chuck his phone across the room, but he knew he couldn't do that. He needed to keep his cool and not let the guys in that something was bothering him. Not that they wouldn't notice.

The lock clicked, so he stood quickly and retreated to the bathroom, hoping to gain some composure before he had to come out and face the guys. He ran chilly water in the sink and splashed his face. As water dripped down his chin, he looked at himself in the mirror. Was he an idiot or what?

Banging on the door had him drying his face quickly and opening it with a jerk. Sosimo jumped back and quirked his eyebrow. Zeke pushed past Sosimo with a shake of his head into the room that seemed smaller with all the guys helping Rafe get the last of the gear up and running.

"Did we get everything lined up?" He strode to the table to help Rafe finish setting up the monitors.

"Easy peasy. Especially since we were just here. I tapped back into the security feeds for the conference room like I did for the charity event and beefed it up a little with a few of our own. The room is right down at the end of the hall. If something were to go down, I could be there in less than thirty seconds." Rafe typed on the keyboard, pulling feed after feed up on the bank of screens as they came on.

"Good. We have thirty minutes until the meeting starts. Sosimo, head on up to Miss MacArthur's room. Jake and Derrick, you guys go take up your positions and keep an eye out. Let us know when you see people coming." Zeke clapped his hands together and rubbed them. They all headed out, except for Rafe, who kept switching to different images on his screens.

"You're okay then? You look a little tense." Rafe

turned in his chair and glanced back at Zeke, who stared at his black screen on his phone.

Zeke jerked and looked up at him. "Yeah, I'm cool."

"Your grumpy attitude wouldn't have anything to do with a certain brown-haired bombshell visiting Samantha, would it?" Rafe tapped on a button, and the feed for the house popped up in the screen's corner.

Zeke scowled at Rafe and tossed his phone onto the bed.

"You know, just because she's talking to Kiki, doesn't mean she's gonna agree to go there. Besides, I'm not quite convinced Kiki has the same motives that her parents and Gregory do." Rafe clicked the end of his pen as he chomped on his gum.

"She can go if she wants. I'll be fine." Zeke stomped to his garment bag and unzipped it with the yank.

"Bull."

Zeke looked up and cocked one eyebrow at Rafe. "You think? How can you be so confident in what I'm thinking?"

"Because you're my brother, and I've been through life with you. You're thinking she'll leave you like Gillian did, but you don't know that. Stop putting your fears on her. She's nothing like Gillian." Rafe pointed his pen at Zeke, his expression firm with determination.

Zeke tossed his suit down on the bed, and his shoulders slumped with a sigh. A thousand boulders had piled up on them in the last fifteen minutes since he looked at that stupid video feed. He knew Rafe was right.

Samantha was nothing like Gillian, nothing at all. But the possibility of her choosing the Paynes had him so bound up with worry that he wasn't sure if he could handle getting any closer to Sam than he had.

He looked at Rafe, who stared him down. "You're right, I shouldn't jump to conclusions."

"Just like always. When are you guys gonna agree I'm always right?" He turned back to the screens, flipping from the house to the feed in the hotel. "You better get ready, Twinkle Toes. Your ball is about to start."

Zeke chucked his socks, beaning Rafe in the back of the head. Zeke laughed loudly as he stripped off his shirt to put on his suit. He had a job to do and needed to remain focused. His phone dinged. He looked down at it, swiping it open quickly when he saw a message from Samantha.

Be safe. Hurry home. I'm praying for you.

His chest eased as he read her message again. He typed a quick response. *Don't worry. We'll be safe. See you soon.*

She quickly replied with a smiley face, and he closed his phone with a smile.

"See, I told you." Rafe typed away on the computer, not looking back at Zeke.

Zeke smiled even bigger as he stripped off his pants and started putting on his suit. Rafe was right. He had nothing to worry about, except maybe the next few hours playing Spy on the Terrorist. He groaned. This meeting was gonna be a blast.

SAM RELAXED on the couch in her apartment, reading a book on her tablet. Well, attempting to read a book. She hadn't swiped the page in the last ten minutes. She had put Eva to bed after they had prepared some snacks for the guys at the main house. Now she wished she had put Eva to bed at the other place instead of coming back to their apartment. She hadn't known a business meeting would last until almost midnight. Maybe she should just go to bed.

She sighed, tossed the device onto the couch, and stared at her reflection in the windows. Her skin no longer stretched across sharp cheekbones. Her hair had gotten its shine back. But more than that, she no longer saw the loneliness and pain that had stared back at her every time she peered in the mirror. She had never imagined it would feel so light without the weight pressing on her.

She thought back to her conversation with Kiki, how Sam had gotten a sense of forlornness from her. Kiki came by to ask if she could visit. Just that, nothing more. The way her parents acted had disgusted her, not understanding where the loving parents of her youth had gone. Sam hadn't answered Kiki's request, but when her mind stopped obsessing over Zeke and the guys for a minute or two, it wondered what it would hurt to let Kiki come to the house to hang out. Maybe Kiki needed to find a sense of family, like Sam had.

She startled when she saw the beams from headlights splash across the meadow. Should she go see if they needed anything? She rolled her eyes. These guys had been on countless missions far more dangerous than a simple business meeting. They didn't need someone mothering them with cookies and snacks. She suddenly felt silly leaving the food out at the other place.

"Well, it's too late now." Sam pushed her curls out of her face as she stood and went to her bedroom window that overlooked the drive and main house.

Sosimo ushered a woman into the house. The way her hair stuck out in all directions, her shoulders slumped as she leaned on Sosimo, made Sam's insides quiver. Something had happened. She glanced at the SUV parked in front of the stables. The light from the open door revealed Zeke scowling up at her apartment before he stomped out of view.

She closed the curtain with a snap. Had she done something to upset him, or was he just mad over the job that had obviously gone wrong? She wasn't sure what to do. She wanted to go see him, but she also didn't want to leave Eva alone.

She paced in her dark bedroom. Maybe she wasn't cut out for a relationship like this. Was she fooling herself that she'd ever feel comfortable with what he did?

She squared her shoulders and went back to the couch. Picking up her phone, she sent Zeke a text.

Is everything okay?

She chewed on her thumbnail. Her jiggling knees about bounced her off the cushion. The ding of her phone caused her to jump.

Yeah. Job went south. We're just cleaning up.

Okay. What did that mean? She relaxed into the back of the couch when she remembered all the gear they had taken.

Is your client okay?

His text popped back almost instantly.

She will be.

She wanted to go talk to him, to see with her own eyes that everything was fine. Something about his brief responses held her back. He probably just had a lot of work to do.

Eva's asleep. I left food for you at the main house.

Should she ask him to stop by when he finished?

Thanks. Good night.

Guess not.

Good night.

Sam stared at her phone. She wished she had someone she could call and talk to. She thought about texting Beatrice, but they were still on their honeymoon. Wouldn't that be awkward. *Hey, Bea. Let me interrupt your amazing trip with some relationship problems of my own.* Sam shook her head. Besides, she got the feeling that Beatrice was even more inexperienced than Sam was in the whole guy department.

She couldn't do much more tonight and fretting wouldn't do her any good. The guys had arrived home. They were all whole and safe. She just needed to leave her worry behind and go to bed. She rose and marched over to the light, flicking it with more force than necessary. Besides, tomorrow would be soon enough for her to talk to Zeke.

CHAPTER THIRTEEN

Zeke growled the next morning as he crossed to the house from the stables. Not only was he exhausted, but his arm ached like the devil. He rolled his shoulder as he marched up the steps.

He had lain awake, going over Sam's conversation with Kiki. He'd also gnawed at the fact she hadn't come out to see him when they arrived, which made him worse than a teenage boy. He could've just as easily gone to see her after he'd gotten stitched up, but he'd been the one to say goodnight.

He flexed his arm. He hadn't wanted to see her because he was more than a little afraid of how she'd react to his injury. It didn't matter that the bullet had just left a crease in his arm. He was the type of man Sam's mom had always warned Sam about. Would she see his injury as a sign and be more willing to pack up and leave? The doubt about what she'd say left his stomach in knots.

So when he had woken up, instead of searching her out, he had focused his time on getting Reagan situated and coming up with a security plan for her. Now, however, he couldn't put off seeing Sam any longer without calling himself a coward. He walked down the hall like he was going to the guillotine.

Would she come out and say that she didn't want to further their relationship? He wondered how they could work together. If he could be near her every day without slowly going insane or begging like a fool to make it work. Maybe he could set up a satellite office somewhere else, say the other side of the world. That's what he'd have to do, because he couldn't stay here if they weren't together, and he couldn't stand the thought of her and Eva unprotected somewhere else.

He paused in the doorway. She sat in her typical position, typing away on the computer with pencils in her ponytail. Everything in him wanted to cross the expanse between them, pull her up, and declare how much he loved her.

He pushed the urge aside and stomped into the office. He slumped in the chair on the other side of the desk from her and grabbed the tennis ball resting on the edge. He fiddled with it, trying to figure out what to say.

"We'll be housing Reagan here for at least a few days until we can figure out a game plan." He squeezed the ball and looked at her across the desk.

Her lips pressed together, and her fingers froze on the keyboard. "She's staying here? Will that be safe?"

"Yeah, she is. That's what this house is for, to shelter people in need." He set the ball on the desk and sat back in the chair. He knew his tone was sharp but couldn't help it.

Sam placed her hands in her lap. "What about the men trying to get her?"

"Rafe's figuring that out." Zeke blew out a breath, seeing her pull back more and more with each word that he spoke. "We'll have the gates locked and all of our alarm systems up and running while she's here. We'll also have 24-hour surveillance, one of us watching the monitors all the time. Nobody will get to her while she's here."

Sam looked out the window, her bottom lip pulling between her teeth as she nodded. "Okay." She looked back at him. Something shone in her eyes he couldn't quite read, chilling him to the core. "I finished inputting all of your past invoices and receipts. Everything should be up to date as of today. It'll be easy to keep up now."

Zeke's palms sweated, and he wiped them on his pants. The more he acted like a jerk, the more closed off she became. He needed to save this conversation, turn it around somehow.

"That's good." Zeke inwardly groaned at his own feeble attempt at dialogue and stood abruptly, pushing the chair back. "Well, I have some things that I need to get set up, so I'd better be going."

"All right." Sam looked back out the window, her chin trembling before she firmed it.

"Listen—"

Sam talked over him. "I think Eva and I will have a quiet night at home this evening."

And there it was, her distancing herself from him.

"All right."

It was anything but all right. Her distance ripped his heart from his chest. He turned and stalked out of the room, wishing he could take the time to go shoot something.

———

SAMANTHA STOOD from her desk with a huff of disgust and paced in front of the office window. She stopped and pushed the heels of her hands against her eyes. What had she just done? She blinked at the sting of tears that threatened to ruin the strong image she'd fought so hard to keep while sitting across from Zeke.

She threw her hands down to her sides and stared out the window. All morning she'd been waiting for him to come talk to her, each minute ticking by at an excruciating pace. Then he showed up all gruff, and what did she do? Returned his gruff with her own negativity.

She knew Reagan needed to be where she was safe. That's what Sam had signed up for when she took this job and moved out here. She needed to go apologize. She turned to rush out the door but skidded to a stop when she thought of Zeke's upset face.

He hadn't come to see her all day long. She hadn't exactly gone out of her way to see him either. Maybe it was for the best. Maybe they both just needed a little bit of space. Everything in the last month had been happening so fast that she felt like she was on her favorite roller coaster at Worlds of Fun back in Kansas City. While she loved the feeling of being tossed this way and that in the safety of the locked seats on the Timber Wolf ride, she hated feeling that way in actual life.

All she ever wanted was a stable life, someone who

came home each night and lived like every other American. It was one reason she was an accountant. Beyond the fact that she loved numbers, it seemed such an ordinary job that only required extra time during tax season. She had never wanted to date someone like her dad, or her mom for that matter, yet here she had fallen in love with someone just as dangerous to her heart.

A growl and giggling screams came through the open window. She glanced down at the yard just as Eva dashed across the drying grass, screaming and laughing in joy. Zeke raced after her, a smile stretched across his face. Sam's heart clenched and a tear she'd worked so hard to keep in broke loose from her eye. This man may not have the boring life of a pencil pusher that she'd always believed she would marry, but he would be there for her and Eva every day if she let him.

"I'll save you, my fairy princess," Rafe hollered across the yard as he took off after Zeke.

Eva squealed even louder and changed course so she was running toward Rafe. "Save me, Rafe. Save me."

Zeke caught up to Eva and snatched her up into his arms, throwing her over his shoulder. "You're mine now."

His words sliced through Sam, almost buckling her knees from beneath her. She backed up against the desk and leaned into it. Why was she fighting this? She had more sense of family here with Zeke and his friends than she ever had anywhere she'd ever lived.

The scene became unfocused through her tears. She quickly blinked them away. When her eyes focused again, Zeke flinched and quickly set Eva down when she kicked his arm in her pretend attempt to escape. What was that about?

Sam stood and rushed out of the office. By the time she got outside and into the yard, Rafe had gotten Eva from Zeke and was flying her around the yard. Zeke's smile vanished the instant he saw Sam.

She walked up to him, though her mind screamed to run away. Red slashed across his sleeve, and she gasped, feeling a little lightheaded. She pointed at the blood soaking through his long sleeved shirt.

"You're bleeding." Really, Genius? He could see that. "I thought you said no one was hurt."

Zeke's eyebrows creased in a confused expression. "No. I believe I said we were all okay. It's just a minor scratch. I probably just pulled it loose."

She grabbed his hand and pulled him toward the stables. "Let's go look at it."

She hated the fact that he didn't thread his fingers through hers, but dropped her hand the instant they started walking. She crossed her arms over her chest and walked quietly beside him. The longer they walked in silence, the thicker the tension became, like taffy stretched thin between them. Each second pulled her further and further from what she thought she'd wanted.

They arrived into the sick bay without saying a single word, and she motioned to the table. "Why don't you take off your shirt?"

He cocked his eyebrow and hid a smirk as he reached for the hem of the shirt. Sam turned toward the cabinets, praying her dark skin hid her embarrassment. She found gauze pads and medical tape and brought them over to the table. Her gaze skittered across Zeke's well-defined body, trying hard not to let her brain turn her into an ogling ninny. As she moved to focus on his arm, her eyes became arrested by a scar high on his collarbone. Without thinking, she ran her finger over the raised, rippled surface and glanced up at Zeke.

"That was a bullet in Afghanistan." Zeke took a deep breath, his chest rising with the action, and let it out slowly.

Samantha touched a long scar down his side. He flinched sideways like it tickled and grabbed her hand.

"What's that one from?" Her voice came out airy.

"Knife fight in Kazakhstan." He threaded his fingers through hers, twisting them as he surveyed their hands clasped together.

The scars were a testament of the danger he had been put in. But they also told the story of his triumphs. Each scar a witness to his determination not just to survive, but to help others.

"I'm sorry." The words trembled out of her mouth.

Zeke tore his gaze from their hands and stared into her eyes. "Me too." His voice was low and thick.

She held his gaze for a long moment, not wanting to break this time. She took a deep breath and softly pulled her hand away. "Let me look at your arm."

He nodded and let her hand go. With trembling fingers, she unwrapped his arm, gasping at a stitched line across his bicep. Blood oozed from the corner that had come loose, and Sam's stomach twisted.

"What happened?" She knew her wide eyes showed her fear.

"A bullet grazed my arm."

She swallowed the pain in her throat and blinked rapidly to keep the tears in her eyes.

"I promise, we had the situation under control," he quickly added and held his hands up to calm her.

"What if it would've been worse? What if—"

Zeke placed his finger on her lips. "None of us know when our last day here on earth is. None of us, not even you. God created me to help people." Zeke ran his fingers down her cheek. "I know this makes you nervous, Sam, but we have something special here. Something I know you feel too."

Sam closed her eyes and exhaled a shuddering breath. She felt it. With every cell in her body, she knew that she would love Zeke for the rest of her life. She just wasn't sure she could handle the pain if he got killed.

"I just don't know. I'm ... I'm not sure I'm strong enough."

Zeke leaned back and nodded, a sadness in his eyes she'd never seen before.

"This just needs a butterfly bandage, and it'll be fine." He shrugged his wounded arm, then pointed to a cabinet. "You can find them in there."

Sam nodded and turned toward the cabinet, willing her knees not to buckle. She opened it and searched the boxes until she found the butterfly bandages. Grabbing a couple, she turned back to Zeke, closed the wound, and rebandaged it. She smoothed the last bit of tape over the bandage, lingering with a soft touch. She swallowed the lump in her throat, knowing if she looked up that she would lose it.

"Shh, it's okay, Sam. Everything's all right." Zeke wiped her face—she didn't even know it was wet with tears—and pulled her close.

He kissed her softly on the lips. Her insides trembled with the tentative touch. She angled her head to deepen the kiss. Snaking her hands behind his back, she pulled him close. She needed to feel the solidness of him. Needed his presence to push away her fear. As she kissed him with an abandon she hadn't before, she tried to force her mind to stop freaking out. But the tighter she held him, the sharper the image of her mom crying out in her sleep. Only this time it wasn't her mom, but herself.

CHAPTER FOURTEEN

Zeke inhaled a deep breath the next morning as he sat on the back porch with a cup of coffee. The frigid autumn night air still lingered and was brisk in his lungs. A pair of ducks quacked loudly on the pond. He hoped they would be there later for him to show Eva.

While things with him and Samantha were still a little strange, the rest of the day, after she had cried in his arms, had seemed less strained. His gut still clenched as he waited for the other shoe to fall, but his darn heart kept pounding its hopeful song that she would prove different from his mom and Gillian.

Tires crunching along the rock drive broke the calm morning air. When no car door slammed and the engine didn't cut off, Zeke placed his cup of coffee on the table and stood to go see who was there. Eva's nanny, Tina, sat in her car, looking wildly around. All of Zeke's years of battle had the hairs on the back of his neck rising. He took off into the house, putting his phone to his ear as he ran.

"Dude, I had last shift. Why're you waking me up?" Rafe's groggy voice came through the speaker.

"Something's wrong. Get the guys and get here, stat." Zeke hung up and skidded to a stop at the driver's side door.

Tina's eyes were wide, and tears rolled down her cheeks. Maybe it was something personal, and he was just overreacting. He was strung so tight at the moment, it wouldn't surprise him if his instincts had fried.

"Tina, open the door." Zeke tried the handle, but it was still locked. She shook her head frantically. "Roll down the window, Tina."

Tina rolled down the window and handed him her phone. "He says he wants to talk to you." Tina's words were barely discernible through her tears.

Zeke grabbed the phone and put it up to his ear.

"I want Reagan." A hard voice came over the phone. "You have thirty minutes."

Silence from the other end met him before he could answer. A ding came across the phone, and he looked at a text message with the emoji of a bomb. Zeke's insides turned to ice.

"Zeke, Tina!" Eva's beautiful voice yelled as she ran up to him and hugged his knee.

Tina's eyes widened and darted to Eva and back to him. He pulled Eva up to his chest and ran to where Samantha was walking up. Her smile quickly changed to a frown as he gave Eva a hug and handed her to Sam.

"I need you to take Eva into the house now. Sosimo will be there in a minute. Go with him into the bunker with Reagan."

"Zeke, what's going on?" Sam's gaze bounced from him to Tina's car and back.

"I'm not entirely sure yet, but I need you guys to be safe." He ran his hand over her cheek, pushing her hair out of her face. "Please, don't ask questions, just go."

"Okay." Samantha darted around him and raced to the house, clinging to Eva.

Zeke breathed out in relief and stomped back over to the car. "What did the man say when you answered, Tina?"

"He said if I turned the car off or got out, I wouldn't live another second. That he wanted to talk to whoever was in charge." Her hands shook as she pushed her hair from her face.

He bent so Tina's focus turned to him, trying to keep her steady until the guys could help him search the car and see if there really was a bomb. "Tina, I need you to remain calm when I tell you what I'm about to say. Can you do that for me?"

Tina's eyes widened, but she nodded.

"Good. The man said there is a bomb, I'm assuming somewhere on your car." Zeke's words caused Tina's breath to hitch and increase. "Slow breaths, Tina. I promise you, we've taken care of things like this a hundred times or more. Don't worry, we'll figure this out."

Rafe's Jeep skidded to a halt next to Tina's car.

"What's going on?" Jake looked into the car as he marched up.

"Got a call from a man saying there's a bomb on Tina's car. He told me to give Reagan up or we would regret it." Zeke turned Tina's phone around so the guys could see the message.

Their eyes went wide. The sound of four men collectively sucking in air would've been funny in any other circumstance.

"Sosimo, get Reagan, Sam, and Eva into the bunker. The rest of us will figure this out. You can watch the monitors from there. If the worst happens, take the tunnel to the old garage and get them to safety."

Sosimo nodded and took off running. The rest of them got busy searching the car. Rafe whistled long and low and sat back from where he peered underneath the car.

"It looks like we have eighteen minutes." Rafe ran his hand over his bedhead hair. He was in a ratty T-shirt and sweats. Nothing like a good, old-fashioned bomb threat to wake one up.

"Does it look to be weight censored?" Zeke bent down to look under the car.

"See how it's taped down?" Rafe lay down on the ground next to him and pointed at the way whoever was after Reagan had attached the bomb.

"It looks like it's just a slap-and-go job." Zeke got back up. "It's safe to get Tina out."

He scanned all the guys' faces. This was what he loved about his family—how well they knew each other and their willingness to jump into any situation. As dangerous as this form of life was, every single one of them wanted nothing more than to help others.

"I'll go get the blast blankets." Derrick took off running for the stables.

Jake nodded. "It could work. If they have someone watching, we'll be in trouble then."

"Well, with the way the house is situated, they won't be able to see." Rafe pointed toward the lengthy drive that wound over a mile through trees.

"Unless they somehow snuck on to the property," Zeke pointed out.

"Not without tripping the sensors." Rafe rubbed his hand down his beard. "They would've never known that they had to go all the way to the back corner twenty miles into the wilderness to get to a spot that didn't have sensors."

Zeke nodded confirmation and pointed at Jake. "Jake, double check what we think. Make sure you don't see something that we're missing. I don't want her to get out and have the thing blow on us." Zeke stepped back and looked at Tina. "Everything's gonna be okay, Tina. We're figuring this out, all right?"

Jake dusted off his hands as he sat up. "I think it's just the simple slap-and-go bomb like you said. Did you see how it's taped to a cell phone that's counting down?" He peeked one last time before standing. "They probably called or texted and started the countdown. We're safe getting Tina inside." He peered around before he shrugged. "If one of you guys are feeling brave, you could always drive it into the field. Let it detonate out there."

Zeke nodded his head. "All right. Let's do this."

Derrick ran up with the bomb protection and started handing it out.

Zeke leaned on the open window. "Tina, this is what we need you to do. When I open the door, you'll jump out into Rafe's arms. He'll spin and land on top of you with the blast blanket, that way, if we're wrong and this detonates, you'll have protection, okay?"

Tina nodded, her lip bottom chin trembling. "Okay." Her voice shook.

"Good. When the bomb doesn't detonate, because we honestly believe it won't, you'll stand up and run to the house with Rafe behind you, okay?"

She nodded again. Zeke turned to the other guys. "Let's get the steering wheel tied off. As soon as she's clear, we wedge the gas pedal and throw it into drive. It should get clear past the pond before it detonates."

"We should have the fire department on call." Derrick pointed toward the field. "Everything is dry out there. When it detonates, we may have a bigger problem on our hands."

"Good idea. Get on it." Zeke turned to Tina. "Are you ready?"

She shook her head. "Yes."

Zeke smiled. "All right, on the count of three, I'll open the door and you jump into Rafe's arms."

"You're the prettiest lady I've had throw herself at me lately." Rafe winked and raised his eyebrows at her. "I won't mind catching you at all."

Tina's cheeks pinked. "I wouldn't be either if it weren't for this dire circumstance."

Tina's deadpan delivery had all the guys laughing. Rafe clutched his heart. She smiled at them all.

"That a girl. Let's get you out of there." Zeke patted her shoulder.

He grabbed the handle and counted down from

three. When he yanked the door open, Tina flew into Rafe's arms, and they all shielded themselves under the blankets. Zeke counted to five, his heart pounding in his throat. When nothing happened, Rafe picked up Tina and ran toward the door.

Zeke quickly weighted the gas pedal down with a brick and wedged a stick against it so it wouldn't move. The engine revved loudly, almost drowning out the thumping of his heart in his ears. He threw the car into drive, jumping back as fast as he could. It rocketed across the field, bumping along the way. He worried that the brick might get dislodged. When it got halfway to the pond, it exploded with such force that Zeke fell to the ground.

He growled as the ducks flew away. Just great. Now he couldn't show Eva the ducks. He hated when his plans got blown out of the water.

CHAPTER FIFTEEN

Sam watched the monitors as Zeke reached for the car
door handle, and Rafe stood with what looked like a
blanket wrapped behind him and his arms held wide.
Her heart hadn't stopped pounding painfully in her chest
since the minute Zeke forced her to run. The fear in his
eyes had been so tangible she'd almost buckled with the
impact of it. When Sosimo had come in and taken them
to the bunker, he'd said that there was a bomb in Tina's
car and turned on the wall of screens with surveillance
feeds. Sam had trouble breathing ever since.

She wanted to close her eyes when Zeke had grabbed
hold of the handle, but she couldn't tear her gaze away
from the monitor. Her entire body had trembled as she
held herself in a hug to keep from flipping out. Sam had
pressed her hand against her lips to keep her shocked sob
in as Zeke reached into the car. It shot off across the yard,
and Sosimo pointed to another screen where they saw the
car heading toward the pond. Without warning, a big fire-
ball filled the screen. The walls of the bunker shook, and

Eva whimpered where she looked through books on the couch.

"Mama?" Her wide blue eyes showed her worry.

"It's okay, honey. Everything will be okay." Sam forced a smile, and Eva went back to looking at the books.

"Hey Eva, can you show me your stories?" Sosimo sat down on the couch, pulled Eva onto his lap, and started reading the book to her.

Sam tore her gaze from her daughter and turned back to the screen. Zeke was on the ground, sitting up, and staring at the car that was now ablaze. Jake and Derrick scrambled to their feet, shaking their heads. How had this even happened? How had Reagan's enemies known to target Tina? Sam looked at Reagan, her heart dropping. This was what life would be like. Sam hugged herself tighter, trying to keep all the shattering pieces of herself held together.

Zeke stood and said something to Jake and Derrick, then took off for the house. Sam twisted her hands and looked back at Eva, who sat happily in Sosimo's lap, staring up at him in love. Could she really keep her here when bombs were being strapped to cars and driven up the driveway? Her eyes pricked with tears, and she blinked them away. Now was not the time for weakness. She had to be strong for Eva's sake.

The bunker door swooshed open, and Zeke stomped in, his gaze scanning everyone before finally landing on her. His shoulders dropped, and he closed his eyes, opening them back up and turning to Sosimo.

"We need to get you and Reagan out here." Zeke was

all business, like a bomb hadn't just blown a hole in his backyard.

Sam moved to the couch, and grabbed Eva from Sosimo's lap. She held Eva tightly and combed her hand over her head. What if the bomb would've gone off when Eva had run up to Zeke? Sam's hand shook as she wrapped her arms more firmly around her daughter.

"I have an idea. I can have it underway in under an hour." Sosimo crossed his arms over his chest, his gaze flicking to Reagan, who stood staring at the screen where the car still sat in flames.

"Figured you would," Zeke said, and Sosimo's shoulders relaxed. "Get the guys on whatever you need for us to support you."

Sosimo nodded then turned to Eva. "Hasta luego, mi burbujita."

Eva launched and hooked Sosimo around the neck. "Te amo."

Sam's throat constricted. She pulled Eva back to her and gave her a kiss on the cheek. Zeke turned his attention to Reagan, and Sam followed Sosimo out the door.

As she walked down the hall, she heard Zeke talking to Reagan. "We'll get you safe and make sure you're able to get in front of the Soldier Enhancement Program."

Sam walked as quickly as she could up the stairs and into the living room. She slowed as she saw the guys gathered around the coffee table, deep in discussion. Tina sat at the kitchen island, shakily drinking some water. Sam hurried to her and gave her a hug.

"Are you okay?" Sam pulled back to look into Tina's face.

Tina smiled and tweaked Eva's nose. "Yeah, I'm fine. Nothing like an explosive morning to get your engines running, right?"

Sam exhaled shakily and adjusted Eva on her hip. "I am so, so sorry."

Tina shrugged. "Who would've thought when I took a job as a nanny, I'd be jumping from cars into the arms of a hunky guy, watching my car blowup?"

"It's definitely not something I ever considered." Samantha shook her head and looked out at the smoke visible through the window. "I'm guessing you're probably going to be looking for a new job now."

"Are you kidding me?" Tina's face lit up despite her shakiness. "This is the most amazing job I've ever had."

Sam startled and stared wide-eyed at the spunky woman. "Well, okay. I think I'll take Eva home for a bit. Why don't you just hang out here and see if they need any help?"

"Absolutely." Tina looked over at the guys with a smile. "Do you think I might be able to learn how to do some of this security stuff?"

"I don't really know. You'll have to talk to Zeke," Sam said as she walked toward the front door.

She hurried out of the house and across the driveway. She scanned the area, her eyes darting this way and that, looking for anyone who could hurt them.

Eva gasped and pointed to the smoldering remains. "Tina's car's on fire."

"Yeah, honey. It had a little problem."

"I'm glad she was here." Eva placed her head back on Sam's shoulder. "So Zeke and the uncles could help her."

Eva's words skidded Sam to a halt. She peered into Eva's face. "Why did you just call them that?"

Eva shrugged. "Some of my friends talk about their uncles at school. And I just thought, with Zeke being your prince, that they would be my uncles now."

Sam's eyes glossed over, and she sniffed. How was she supposed to tell her daughter that this wasn't her family? That they weren't safe here? She hugged Eva close and practically ran the rest of the way to their apartment, slamming the door behind them.

She put Eva down and leaned against the door. "Eva, I need you to go pack your backpack."

Eva's forehead furrowed, and she shook her head. She knew what that meant—had been told the same thing too many times to count the last few months.

"But I want to stay here." Eva's chin trembled, and Sam almost lost control of her own tears.

"I know, honey, but it's not safe here." Sam put her hand on Eva's shoulder.

Eva wrenched away and crossed her arms. "It is, too, safe here. Zeke and the uncles will keep us safe."

Samantha shook her head. "Honey, you don't understand what's going on. Listen and obey, and go pack your bag." She hadn't had to use that tone of voice with Eva often. It usually got her jumping, but this time she just glared at up at Sam.

"I don't want to."

"You don't have a choice." *And neither do I.* She grabbed Eva's arm and walked her back to her bedroom, pointing at her bag. "Pack up what you want. We'll be leaving soon."

Sam turned and walked out of the bedroom as Eva's cries filled the air. She knew their sound echoed the breaking of her own heart. She had to be strong though if she was to keep Eva safe.

She rushed into her room and threw things into her suitcase and gym bag. The action was so reminiscent of four weeks earlier that she almost laughed at the thought. Then, she had believed that she would finally be safe. That she could finally breathe, even if it was just for a while. She never imagined that her life would spiral so out of control. This was what happened when you opened your heart to a man. She'd known better.

She hauled her suitcase and bag into the living room. A knock on the door kicked her heart into overdrive. Zeke's voice called through the wooden barrier. Her stomach twisted. She closed her eyes and clenched her fists.

Eva ran full speed down the hall, opening the door before Sam could move. "Zeke, make her stop. Make her stay," Eva cried as he lifted her up.

His eyes widened in shock, then narrowed as he peered over at Sam and her suitcases. "What's going on?"

"We can't stay here. It's not safe." Sam crossed her arms, holding in the desire to run to him and let him push away all of her fears.

"Sam, please, let's talk about this." He stepped forward, reaching out as Eva buried her face into his neck.

Sam laughed without humor. "What is there to talk about? A car blew up in the backyard, Zeke. How can you say that we'll be fine? I can't keep Eva here where she might have to watch one of you guys be blown to smithereens." Her voice rose with each word. She took a deep breath to calm down. "Eva, go finish packing your backpack. We're leaving."

Eva clung tighter to Zeke. He stared into Sam's eyes. Then he flicked a switch, and a shield of indifference replaced the pain shining there. He placed Eva down and pushed her hair out of her face.

"You need to listen to your mom, squirt." Zeke's voice was strained with emotion.

"But Zeke—"

"No buts, Eva. Your mom wants you to go pack your backpack, so you better do it."

Eva's face crumpled as tears streamed down her cheeks. She spun and ran to her room, shoving Sam as she went by.

"I hate you!" Eva's words knifed into Sam's heart.

Sam closed her eyes and shuddered out a breath. She opened them to find Zeke staring at her.

"So this is it?" His hands clenched into fists by his side.

Sam nodded, and he looked out the window, his lips pressed together in a line.

Her voice stuttered over the tightness in her throat. "I can't ... I can't have my heart broken like my mom did. I can't lose somebody again."

"You don't get to choose when you lose people, Sam." Zeke's voice was low and sad. "This life doesn't give us guarantees like that."

Sam nodded even though he wasn't looking. "I know."

He turned his anguished gaze to her, penetrating into her soul. "Do you?"

Sam pulled her bottom lip in between her teeth and bit down hard, trying to keep from crying. She shook her head and turned down the hall to get Eva. Eva had shoved all of her toys into her backpack and sat crying on the floor. Sam bent down and picked her up, whispering apologies into her ear. After throwing Eva's clothes into a bag, Sam dragged her feet back out to the living room.

Zeke already stood at the door, holding it open, her suitcases in his hands. She swallowed the lump in her throat and walked solemnly out of the apartment and down the steps to the garage. She got to her car and buckled Eva into her booster while Zeke put her bags in the trunk. She gently closed the door and opened hers, knowing if she didn't put some distance between them, she'd lose her determination to leave.

He stepped close. "Where will you go?"

"I don't know," Sam whispered.

Zeke nodded and reached his hand up toward her face only to close it, then shove it into his pocket. "When you figure out what you want to do, give Rafe a call. He can get you papers for a new life. Exactly what you're wanting."

"Zeke—"

Zeke stepped away and moved toward the garage door. He stared at her as the door opened.

"Keep low and stay safe," he said as he held his hand over the garage door button.

She swallowed the rock in her throat and nodded. "You, too."

She sank into her car and started the engine, glad that Sosimo had fixed everything wrong with it. Just another testament of how well she had been taken care of the last few weeks. She put the car in drive and pulled slowly out of the garage, keeping her eyes forward so she couldn't see Zeke's face. Eva sobbed in the back seat, banging her hand against the window as they drove out the door.

Sam told herself not to look in the rear-view mirror, but her heart pulled her eyes up. Zeke stood, staring after them, his arms across the chest. Before she dragged her gaze from the mirror, she saw him swipe his hand across his cheek. Her heart, that she had held so carefully together, shattered into a million pieces onto the rusty floorboard.

CHAPTER SIXTEEN

The next morning, Sam rushed across the train depot, aiming for the two empty seats she saw next to the window. The light shone on them in a way that gave the illusion of hope. She needed all the hope she could get. Their night had been horrible at the hotel, with Eva crying and whining long into the night until she had fallen asleep with her cheeks moist with tears. The pattern had picked up the minute the child had woken up, but Sam had a plan.

She remembered the waitress saying the train left at 12:10 p.m. every day, heading toward Denver, so she'd researched the night before and decided heading toward Denver wouldn't be a terrible idea. The plan killed two birds with one stone. Not only would the Paynes not expect her to move closer to them, but it gave Sam a way to bribe Eva into cooperating that morning. Since she couldn't trust her car to get her to the next town, she figured when she got wherever she ended up, she'd find another vehicle. Zeke had certainly paid her enough to start over.

So while Eva skipped toward the window to watch for the train to arrive, Sam's heart broke a little more. She sat with a slump and sighed heavily. She didn't think it would be this hard. She never imagined the memory of Zeke would saturate every thought.

"Mama, look. You can see the bridge where we walked with Zeke the other day." Eva pointed out the window at the footbridge across the Colorado River.

The image of Zeke holding Eva's hand and swinging her in between the two of them slammed into Sam. She closed her eyes to escape the memory. That was a mistake. His smile he had kept so long from her filled her vision the same as it had her dreams.

She swallowed hard and then peered down at Eva. "Yeah, honey, I see that."

She didn't understand how every place she looked at and every thought seemed to turn back to Zeke. It wasn't like they had gone very many places besides the ranch. But she'd see someone with dark brown hair and remember how his had been soft beneath her fingers. She'd hear an SUV fire up somewhere and think about riding up the mountain to Chase and Beatrice's wedding. He'd been so standoffish, yet, at the same time, protecting her. Even when he wasn't thrilled with her, he always went out of his way to do what was best for her and Eva.

Then, to make matters worse, what he said to her in the apartment assaulted her mind repeatedly like a battering ram. He was right. She didn't get to choose when people left her or died. Her mom had admonished her not to love a man intent on putting himself in danger, yet she ended up dying on her way home from the hospital in a car crash. Sam couldn't control when the people she loved died. She'd only make herself sick with worry if she tried. She had to leave that in God's hands.

She could go out and find herself some guy who worked in the safety of an office building, and he could die going to the grocery store. So why was she so stuck on what Zeke did? Hadn't he proven that he would do anything to keep others safe? And she knew, because of what had happened the day before, that he and the guys would figure out even more ways to make the ranch secure.

She looked down at Eva's excited face pressed against the window, glancing up and down the track. With Sam taking off on her own, she had put Eva in even more danger. Sure, Sam could protect her if someone attacked head on, but she couldn't be with her all the time. Especially now that she'd have to find another job somewhere and put her back in daycare.

She should be basking in the relief of leaving, but she was wallowing in the pit of pain she'd created for herself. She pulled her purse against her and wrapped her arms around it, not knowing what to do. Would Zeke even want her back? She understood why he had been so hot and cold to her but didn't know how he truly felt. After what his mom and Gillian had done, she doubted he would even want to look at her if she came groveling to his door.

The train whistle blared in the distance, causing her to flinch and her stomach to bottom out. The time had come for her to decide, and she wasn't any closer to knowing which way to go. Eva jumped up and down as the train pulled into the depot, her shining smile big for the first time since the morning before. Could Sam really take Eva away from the family that she'd grown to love so much? Sam closed her eyes and inhaled a shaky breath. When she opened her eyes, she blinked away the sting her tears created and rubbed the burn from her nose.

Standing, she reached out her hand and cleared the emotion stuck in her throat. "Let's go. It's time to get on the train."

Eva glanced up and down the tracks one last time, then turned with a deep sigh. Sam swung her hand playfully, hoping to lighten her daughter's mood. Eva's shoulders slumped even further, and Sam knew nothing would work to help her daughter understand. She couldn't blame her since she didn't understand herself. Sam rubbed her hand across her forehead. The intercom announced boarding for the train to Denver. With a frigid feeling throughout her body, she tugged Eva toward the line, wondering if she'd ever be able to fill the gaping hole that was ripping deeply in her heart.

ZEKE SLUMPED ON THE COUCH, staring absently out the window. He slowly twisted Eva's stuffed frog in his hands, the pain in his chest almost unbearable. How had he let his guard down? In such a brief time, Sam and her daughter had needled their way into his very soul, which at the moment felt like it was splitting from his body.

He looked down at the stuffed animal and stared into its big glassy eyes. "So, what do you think I should do?" Was he really talking to a stuffed animal?

"Ugh." Rafe stomped into the room, pulling on his hair. "This sucks, man." He slumped into the other side of the couch, a mirror image of Zeke's posture.

Zeke nodded and set the frog on the coffee table. He had said little to the guys the day before, just that Sam had left for Eva's safety. They hadn't fussed much, but the solemn frowns and deep sighs he heard all night long were reflections of the discontent he felt inside.

Derrick traipsed to the kitchen from the office and opened the cabinet, pulling out Eva's princess cup and twisting it in his big hands. "The place sure is a lot quieter without her here."

The door shot open, and Zeke and Rafe startled from their slumps. Jake stomped in and slammed the door behind him. He scowled the entire distance of his walk to the armchair where he sat, rigid.

"Fix this." Jake pointed at Zeke.

"What do you mean 'fix this'?" Zeke leaned his elbows on his knees. "If Sam doesn't want to be here, I'm not gonna make her."

"That's bull, and you know it." Jake sat back in his chair. "You're just afraid."

"I'm not—" Zeke's words strangled in his throat as Jake raised his eyebrow. "You're right, I am afraid. What if I go to her, and she still doesn't want to come back?" Zeke hated the vulnerability in his voice.

"What if you don't go get her, and she would've said yes?" Jake murmured.

"What if she comes back and then decides later that it's still too dangerous? That would be harder than if I just let them leave now." Zeke ran his hand over his head.

"Man, life is full of what-ifs. You just have to trust God to lead your heart and stop second-guessing." Derrick leaned up against the kitchen table, putting his hands in his pockets. "So the question is, what do you feel God is telling you to do?"

Zeke exhaled deeply and closed his eyes. He'd been praying nonstop since Sam left, but mainly for God to take away the pain and to keep Sam and Eva safe. He never once asked what God's direction was.

Lord, You know the hurt of my heart. You know my fear, but You also know how much I love Sam. How much I want to be Eva's dad. What would You have me do?

As the prayer ended, he thought again of Sam and Eva, and a sense of family exploded in his heart. With it came a sense of peace.

He opened his eyes and glanced between the guys. "I'm gonna go get them."

"I knew you'd get it through your thick skull that you aren't supposed to let her go." Rafe pulled out his phone while he slapped Zeke on the back. "I've triangulated her location to the train station."

Zeke stood as he looked at his watch. "12:10." Zeke's voice came out a soft whisper.

"What was that?" Derrick straightened and took his hands out of his pockets.

"The waitress said the train to Denver leaves at 12:10 p.m. every day." Zeke rushed toward the garage.

"You've got forty-five minutes to get into Glenwood and get through town." Jake's holler followed him into the hall.

"Don't screw this up." Rafe's command was the last thing Zeke heard as he rushed into the garage and fired up the Bronco.

He would not screw this up. He would do whatever he had to do to have Sam and Eva as part of his family. Because no matter what she thought, no matter what their fears were, their love was much stronger than their obstacles. Zeke slammed the pedal to the floor, praying the traffic would clear so he could bring his family home.

CHAPTER SEVENTEEN

Sam squeezed Eva's hand as they stood outside the station, waiting for passengers to finish unloading. The large number of people milling about surprised her. She'd never imagined train travel would be so popular. With a ticket to Denver costing less than a hundred dollars, she supposed it was an affordable alternative to flying. Plus, the views through the mountains were bound to be stunning.

The disembarking passengers thinned to a trickle. Sam's stomach rolled, making her glad she'd skipped breakfast. Eva's hand became heavy in hers. Her daughter's shoulders slumped as if her backpack weighed a million pounds. She gazed down at the ground, her curly hair hiding her sweet face. Shoot. The excitement of the train hadn't lasted as long as Sam had hoped.

A single tear tracked down Eva's freckled cheek, leaving a circle in the pavement. Sam swallowed the pain in her throat as another tear silently slid over Eva's smooth skin. Sam almost wished for the wailing of the night before over Eva's silent agony that communicated Sam's own heart.

Sam pushed Eva's curls back. "Honey, I know this is sad, but we'll find a new place that you'll like just as much." The lie tasted like wet sawdust and clogged her throat.

"No, I won't." Eva hiccupped, the tears falling more freely. "It won't have Zeke or my uncles."

Sam pressed her lips together, her eyes filling with tears. She looked up, hoping to keep them contained, then glanced at the train. Could she do this? Could she rip her daughter's heart out, along with her own, for an empty guarantee of safety and love without pain?

"Come on. Let's get going." Sam gulped down her doubt and pulled Eva toward the train.

A cold wind whipped through the canyon, magnifying the already frigid state of Sam's existence. That she'd been cold since she'd driven from the ranch made her wonder if she'd ever be warm again. A voice calling her name played on the wind, toying with her heart and slowing her feet. Now even nature had turned cruel. The whistle blew, startling her from her silliness. She shook her head and picked up her pace.

"—antha!" She thought she heard as the whistle stopped.

Eva pulled on her hand. "Mama?"

Sam stumbled and turned toward the street. Zeke pushed his way through the crowd on the steps. Spots swam in her vision as her lungs released their constrictive grip on her in a whoosh.

"Zeke." Eva's happy scream shook the remaining cold from Sam.

A large group of older folks with oversized luggage blocked his way down. He vaulted the railing and rushed down the landscaped hill. Eva jumped up and down, squealing, and took off toward Zeke. Sam tried to follow, but her feet refused to move.

Eva threw herself at Zeke. While he caught her and pulled her close, his gaze never wavered from Sam's. He stalked up to her with such focus, his jaw set and his stare penetrating, that Sam's knees almost buckled beneath her. Her body liquefied in the warmth that rushed through her. He stepped close, invading her space and surrounding her with his grounding scent.

"Samantha," he breathed, his palm spreading across Eva's back before he put her down. "I need to talk to your mom, squirt."

Eva nodded, her hands covering her smiling mouth as she took a step back. Zeke stepped closer to Sam, erasing all but inches between them. He reached for her hand, staring into her eyes as he lifted her hand and pressed it flat over his heart. It pounded like a jackhammer against her palm.

"Do you feel that?" His question was quiet, her own heartbeat drumming in her ears, almost drowning it out.

She nodded, her throat so dry she doubted her words would form. "I feel it."

"It stopped when you left. Just refused to beat anymore." He ran his hand over her cheek, tucking her hair behind her ear. "In fact, everything stopped working the instant you drove away. I thought I could push through it. Kept telling myself I'd eventually be able to function without a heart." He took a deep breath and leaned his forehead to hers. "But that's not what I want."

Sam swallowed, the tears she'd been able to control springing back to life. "What do you want?"

"You. I want you, Samantha Jones. I want a life with you. I want to be Eva's dad and have a house full of joy and happiness."

She let out a gasp. Her body filled with helium and threatened to float away. So she did the only thing that seemed rational. She threw her arms around Zeke's neck and held on for all she was worth. She held nothing back in her kiss, pouring all her relief and love into it.

She leaned back enough to whisper on his lips. "I love you."

His smile on her lips was like drinking sunshine. "I love you, too."

She pulled him close and kissed him again. She would not worry about tomorrow or her fears anymore. Having even a day in Zeke's arms far outweighed a lifetime without him.

ZEKE'S HEART beat so much like a 50 Cal in his chest in that moment, he thought it would explode. Death by overwhelming joy sounded like a magnificent way to go. He slid his thumb along Sam's smooth chin and stared into her hazel eyes. He kissed her again, relishing the warmth of her lips that spread to his fingers and toes. Life was back in balance.

"What do you say we go get some lunch, squirt?" Zeke looked down, his gut clenching at the space where Eva had been standing.

Zeke dropped his arms and quickly scanned the area, looking for the daughter of his heart. How could he have been so foolish to get distracted? Zeke spied her rainbow backpack turning the corner at the top of the stairs and bolted in the direction he last saw her.

"Eva," he shouted as he took the stairs two at a time, pushing tourists and bystanders aside. He would get to her if it took every ounce of strength he had. Sam's footsteps slapped loudly right behind him.

Ahead, Gregory Payne pulled Eva to a black sedan parked on the side of the road. Zeke was close, but he wouldn't be able to get there in time. His mind scrambled for alternatives, and he went with the only one that persisted in his mind.

"Stop! Kidnapper!" he yelled, the people on the street stopping with the shout and pointing. "Gregory, stop! You aren't gonna get away with this."

Gregory spun in front of the car and held Eva's back tight against him. Zeke stopped a few feet away, his hands slicked wet with sweat. Eva's cheerful eyes were shrouded in confusion.

"Zeke? Mr. Greg said he wanted to show me his puppy." Eva forehead furrowed as she looked up at Gregory. "He said you wouldn't mind."

"You know Mr. Greg, squirt?" Bile rose up Zeke's throat.

What would Gregory do if Zeke grabbed for Eva? Could he risk it? While one of Gregory's hands held Eva to him with the backpack straps, he kept the other hand hidden. Could he have a weapon that would hurt Eva?

"Yep. He came and played at the school before I stopped going. His son will go there soon." Eva smiled back at Zeke.

Zeke focused on Gregory, attempting to keep his voice light. "So, you're just going to take her?"

Gregory shrugged as he took a step back toward the car door. "I have a lot riding on this."

Zeke's eyes narrowed, following him. "What is that supposed to mean?"

"If I bring Eva to my uncle and aunt, I gain Garrett's control in the family businesses. I can't let that go away because of sentimentality."

"So you'd take a child from her mom for your own gain, not caring about them one bit?"

"You're new to your money. You'll find out soon enough that emotion has nothing to do with maintaining a certain livelihood." Gregory's words curdled in Zeke's stomach.

Zeke clenched his fists to keep from walking up and slamming Gregory in his face. He hid his shock when Sam appeared behind Gregory. She must have circled around somehow without him realizing she was there. Zeke's lip twitched, relief overwhelming his fear. She nodded at him and pointed to Eva.

Zeke smiled a secret smile, and anticipation welled in this gut. "You're right, I don't understand that. But you also fail to understand the ferocity of a mother's love when it's pushed against the wall."

Gregory's arms loosened slightly as confusion crossed

his face. Samantha stepped up behind him and tapped his shoulder. When he turned, Zeke jumped forward and snatched Eva from his arms. He quickly stepped back and held her close to his chest.

"Mommy!" Eva turned toward Gregory.

Sam whacked the side of Gregory's head with her palm, knocking him sideways. Eva gasped and buried her face in Zeke's neck. Gregory shook his head and stood up quickly, coming at Sam with his hands up in a boxer stance.

"You think I won't hit you because you're a girl?" Gregory sneered.

"Oh, I doubt a coward like you wouldn't have any issue with hitting a woman." Samantha looked so fierce and confident, Zeke fell a little more in love than he already was.

Zeke chuckled. Gregory didn't know what he was in for. As Gregory came up swinging, Sam smirked and hit him with her killer thrust. The sight of his head snapping back and him dropping like a fallen tree brought more satisfaction to Zeke's heart than was probably right.

Applause filled the air from the bystanders. Sam smiled over at Zeke and shrugged.

A thump, thump sounded on the side of the sedan door. Zeke sighed as he looked at Sam. He just wanted to get his family home, maybe watch a movie or play chase.

Sam stepped up to him and reached for Eva, moving behind him for protection. It was nice to know that even though she could handle herself and Eva, she trusted him with their safety.

"Mommy, why'd you hit Mr. Greg like that?"

"He wasn't a nice man, Eva," Sam whispered as she gazed at Zeke.

Zeke reached for the door and pulled it open. His mouth dropped. Kiki had her hands bound behind her back and a gag tied around her mouth. A rope hung from one of her ankles, and her feet were showing bruises through her pantyhose. Zeke quickly grabbed the rope and untied it from her ankle. Bending down to where Gregory moaned, Zeke tied the jerk's hands behind his back. Zeke then took the gag from Kiki's mouth and tied that around Gregory's feet.

"What happened?" Zeke leaned in to help Kiki to the edge of the car's seat as sirens sounded down the street.

"I overheard him talking to my parents." Kiki sniffed, her eyes swollen and red from crying.

Zeke untied her hands. She rubbed her wrists that had been rubbed raw and gingerly placed her hand on a cheek that sported a nasty bruise. She shuddered.

"They were talking about taking Eva." Kiki glanced between him and Sam, strength and anger burning from her. "I couldn't let them do that. So I tried to take him down." She snorted a deprecating laugh. "We see how well that turned out."

"Your parents were in on this?" It surprised Zeke she didn't just let Gregory take the blame.

"Yes." Shame filled her eyes before she lowered her gaze. "They knew exactly what Gregory would do. Encouraged it."

"There's no way to prove that." Sam tightened her arms around Eva.

"I'll testify." Kiki's big, blue eyes that were a perfect match to Eva's shone with determination.

Zeke turned his shocked gaze on her.

"It's not right what they tried to do." Kiki nodded as the first officer came on the scene.

"I'm so glad you're okay." After placing Eva down, Sam bent and hugged Kiki. "I want you to come stay with me and Eva for a while."

Sam turned questioning eyes up at Zeke. He nodded, knowing his complicated family had just gotten more tangled. Eva pulled on his hand, and he swung her up into his arms. Sunshine burst into his chest as she snuggled her cold nose into his neck. It was a good thing he didn't like life to be easy.

CHAPTER EIGHTEEN

Warmth rushed through Sam as she pulled under the gate and followed Zeke's Bronco up the drive. She still couldn't believe the crazy tale Kiki had told but was glad she and Zeke had stopped Gregory before he escaped. After Kiki had given her statement and waved off the medics, they had caravanned to her hotel so she could grab her things. She sat slumped against the passenger door, staring absentmindedly out the window.

The drive had been silent, thanks to Eva's insistence that she ride with Zeke, but Sam didn't mind. The time gave her mind a moment to process all that the future seemed to hold. She still tingled from Zeke's mind-blowing kiss and couldn't wait to find a minute to slip away and share another. She darted her eyes to Kiki as her neck warmed. She'd have to try harder to control her thoughts, otherwise she'd look like a lovesick teenager. She smiled, lovesick about summed it up. She shrugged. Who cared if everyone knew? They pulled around the circle drive and stopped in front of the house.

While the mansion was still stunning and took her breath away, it now just felt like home.

"Welcome to the Silver Wolf Ranch." Sam turned to Kiki as the men barreled out of the front door followed by Tina. "The most crazy, amazing place you'll ever be."

Kiki's eyes widened before she looked at her hands twisting in her lap. "Why are you doing this?" Her voice was strained and thick with emotion. "After what my family did to yours ..."

Sam glanced out the window as Rafe swung Eva out of the Bronco, tossing her high in the air. Joyful shrieks competed with low laughs. Eva wrapped her arms around Rafe's neck, kissed him on the cheek, and then scurried down. She made her way to each of her uncles for a similar greeting, chattering the entire time. Sam imagined this family was an odd looking one, but maybe because her experience was measly, she couldn't imagine a better one to be a part of.

"You know, we can't help what our parents do. My mom hid her pain and fear over losing my father by working nonstop. She was rarely home for me." Sam glanced at Kiki with a half-smile, trying to suppress her chuckle. "Yours are kidnapping criminals. But we don't have to follow our parents' examples." She pointed at the chaos, her smile growing large. "I'm choosing family and love over fear, and that family includes you, if you want." She reached over the console and grasped Kiki's clenched hands. "Today you stepped off your family's path. You risked your life to save Ev—"

"No, not really."

"Yes. You didn't know what Gregory would do, but

you attacked anyway." Sam pulled her hand back and grabbed her purse. "You're walking free now, picking your own way. I just hope you let us be a part of your journey. Eva needs an aunt. She obviously has an abundance of uncles." They both laughed as Sam opened her creaking car door, stood, and cupped her hands over her mouth to be heard over the clamor. "Derrick, come give Kiki a hand."

"What? No, I can walk." Kiki scrambled to unbuckle herself.

Sam bent down. "What's the point of having gorgeous men with big muscles around if you can't take advantage of said muscles from time to time?"

"But, I—"

Sam grew serious. "Kiki, I saw your feet and how you limped at the hotel."

Kiki bit her bottom lip, her blue eyes bright with tears.

Sam smiled, hoping to ease her new friend's discomfort. "Let Derrick help you. Besides, these guys are all about rescuing the damsel in distress. It's good now and then to let them feed into that hero ego they've all got."

"What about a hero?" Derrick opened Kiki's door.

"Kiki was a hero today, attacking Gregory and trying to keep him from getting Eva." Sam almost laughed as Kiki's face bloomed a brilliant shade of red. "Her feet are toast after banging on the car door, trying to get loose after the jerk tied her up and gagged her."

Derrick bent down and reached for Kiki's feet, which were so swollen they couldn't fit into her shoes. She sucked in a breath as his big, dark hand wrapped around her skinny ankle. Derrick glanced up, his eyebrows pinched together.

"We have some stuff I can put on these to help. We get a lot of bruises around here, so you'll fit right in." Derrick's words warmed Sam's heart.

When he scooped Kiki up, her wide eyes darted to Sam. She winked and wiggled her eyebrows as Derrick turned to the house. The warmth of a hand spreading across Sam's back lit her insides into a roaring bonfire. She turned as Zeke closed her car door and placed her palm over his heart. He bent and pressed a quick but heated kiss on her lips.

"I missed you." Zeke's low whisper tickled her neck where he lightly kissed.

"It's been like fifteen minutes." Her jest fell short with her lack of air.

"Too long."

He pushed her against the car and captured her lips in a passionate kiss. She laughed against his mouth as she speared her hands through his hair and held him close. Love burned so hot she thought it might consume her. She realized life didn't hold any guarantees, yet life with Zeke, no matter how long God gave her, promised to be one worth fighting for.

ZEKE PACED the apartment's living room as he waited for Sam to finish getting ready. He stopped and picked up Eva's stuffed animal frog and turned it over in his hands. A smile stretched across his face as he thought of all the last two months had brought. Though he never would consider life a fairytale, he now believed in happily ever afters.

He scoffed at himself and tossed the frog prince on the couch. He turned to stare out the windows and crossed his arms. The leaves had all fallen from the trees, and the biting cold of winter had settled into the Colorado Mountains. He huffed and uncrossed his arms, tapping them on his legs nervously.

"Come on. We're going to be late." He pushed his hand through his hair, knowing that it was a ridiculous statement since all they had to do was walk across the driveway. But this Christmas celebration felt like no other he had before.

"I'm almost ready." Sam's voice floated down the hall, picking up Zeke's already frantic heartbeat.

If he didn't get a hold of himself, he was liable to screw this entire thing up. He looked out the window again and smiled as a mule deer bounded across the snow-covered field.

"Okay, I'm ready now." Samantha's words snapped Zeke's gaze back down the hall.

His heart stopped beating, then kicked back up so rapidly his head felt woozy, and he worried he'd passed out. Her beauty took his breath away, and he wondered if maybe there was some truth to the fairytales being real.

"You're beautiful." His voice barely leaked out through his dry throat.

Her smile was soft and her eyes twinkled in mirth as she stepped close to him. "You're not so bad yourself," she whispered against his lips before kissing him.

He wrapped his arms around her and pulled her close. He worried he'd muss her up but also wondered if that wouldn't be such a terrible idea. Her laughter bubbled up her chest, and he felt it vibrate against him. She pushed away and smiled up at him.

"We're going to be late." She kissed him gently and stepped away.

"So." He grabbed her and pulled her back, kissing her one more time.

She swatted him on the shoulder, her laughter settling in his stomach. She grabbed his hand and pulled him toward the door. He threaded his fingers through hers, marveling at how her small ones fit perfectly in his. After helping her put on her coat, they walked to the main house in comfortable silence.

He opened the door, and familiar chaos greeted them. The warm smells of Christmas dinner cooking met his nose as laughter and chatter barraged his hearing. Eva sat on Chase's lap, chattering to him and Beatrice about horses. Derrick and Rafe were laughing in the kitchen as they checked on dinner. Kiki and Tina sat at the table, engrossed in something on Tina's phone. Verne and Zeke's father stood at the fireplace, deep in conversation. His stepmother Jodi had cornered Jake, probably pushing essential oils on him.

Sosimo was still back east with Reagan. Zeke felt guilty that Sos couldn't be here. When Zeke had called Sosimo earlier, he'd been fine with missing out. Promised he'd be at the next family celebration. Zeke's heart felt as if it would pound out of his chest with happiness. Zeke helped Sam out of her coat and a whistle sounded in the room.

"Mama, you look like a princess." Eva jumped off the couch and rushed up to them.

Sam hugged Eva against her legs with one hand as she grabbed Zeke's other. His eyes stung, and he blinked them rapidly.

"Hey. What's with the fancy dress?" Rafe whistled low as he pointed up and down at Sam.

Zeke gazed down at Sam. "It's a good thing Verne is here, because we're getting married."

The room exploded into cheers and whistles as Eva threw her arms around his legs. Everyone crowded around them, giving hugs and slaps on backs, some jostling him harder than necessary. He knew that today would be one he would cherish forever. As Verne got the ceremony underway, Zeke stood in front of the windows that overlooked the pond and snow-tipped Rocky Mountains, holding to Sam's hands. He peered down into her eyes that shone with love for him and decided that fairytales absolutely existed.

EPILOGUE

Three Years Later

Zeke leaned against the doorjamb, the sounds of rowdy fun filtering down the hall behind him. Sam sat behind the desk, tapping away at the computer, a pencil stuck in her fancy up-do she'd taken an hour to create. He stifled a smile, his chest heating in happiness. She'd acted slightly crazy the last few days, cleaning the floorboards of their home and forcing him to scrub grout until it shined so white it was blinding. Building a small house on the property had been the smartest idea he'd had since they married. He couldn't imagine what she'd be like in a bigger place.

"Honey, dinner's about to be served." His soft words caused her to jump and a look of being caught red-handed crossed her face. He chuckled as he crossed to her. "You don't want to miss out on Sosimo's turkey and mashed potatoes. You've been looking forward to that all week."

"I know, I know. I just thought of something for our

Honolulu office, and I wanted to make sure I got it down before I forgot." She clicked twice on the computer, closed the screen, and leaned back in the office chair.

Her forehead scrunched as she rubbed her hand low on her round belly. She had cried earlier about looking fat and ugly, but he honestly couldn't remember her ever looking more beautiful. Well, that wasn't true. She'd looked gorgeous on their wedding, and she took his breath away every morning he opened his eyes to her curled up beside him.

"Can you believe how big we've grown in the last three years?" She leaned her head back and closed her eyes.

Zeke rubbed her tight belly before leaning against the desk. "You've grown big, that's for sure. Big and beautiful."

She cracked one eye open, her mouth pinching in a cute pout. "That's not what I meant, and you know it." She opened her other eye and sighed. "Our Hawaii office seems off to a great start. I wish we could go back out there for a visit."

He leaned forward and kissed her softly on the lips, pulling the pencil from her hair. "Soon enough, love." He kissed her again and grabbed her hands. "Come on. Let's get you and Barrett Ethan some turkey."

She laughed as he pulled her up, then cringed and placed her hand on her belly.

"Are you all right?"

"I think Sophie Rose wants some mashed potatoes." She smirked up at him.

Zeke shook his head and tweaked her nose. "We

already have two daughters. This one's gonna be a boy. I can feel it."

He pulled her into the hallway as Eva ran toward them with Claire toddling behind her. Eva slowed and kissed her mama's belly, murmuring to her baby brother. He'd convinced at least one person of his thoughts. When Claire looked to be ready to run headfirst into Sam's legs, he swooped her up into his arms. She squealed and laughed as she twisted from his tickling fingers. His family's laughter filled the hall and his heart with joy he never imagined possible.

As Zeke held his daughter close and led his family to the living room, he realized that if he hadn't fallen for Samantha, he'd still be empty, rattling around the ranch alone though his friends surrounded him. She'd changed everything. The house full of celebrating family and the baby about to be born was a testament of how full his life had become. His heart warmed as he wrapped his free arm around Samantha's waist and kissed her softly on the lips.

Want to know what happens after Sosimo and Reagan escape? I'd love to give you *Capturing Sosimo* for signing up for my newsletter where you'll get exclusive deals, giveaways, and news. Grab your FREE copy and continue the adventure today!

ALSO BY SARA BLACKARD

It was a mission like any other ... until it blew apart around them.

When the Army's Special Ops team is tasked with infiltrating the Columbian jungle and rescuing a kidnapped State Department family, the mission seems like every other one they've executed. But as the assignment unravels, not only is the mission's success at stake, but all the brothers-in-arms leaving the jungle alive hangs in the balance.

Mission Out of Control is the prequel short story for both Vestige in Hope and the Stryker Security Force Series. www.sarablackard.com

ABOUT THE AUTHOR

Sara Blackard has been a writer since she was able to hold a pencil. When she's not crafting wild adventures and sweet romances, she's homeschooling her five children, keeping their off-grid house running, or enjoying the Alaskan lifestyle she and her husband love.

CPSIA information can be obtained
at www.ICGtesting.com
Printed in the USA
BVHW081233120122
625988BV00009B/761